She did not ~~...~~
anything bu ~~...~~

Like the obedient ~~...~~
imagined she was not.

And then everything seemed to speed up again. The priest was going on in Italian. Lionel was responding. Geraldine was beginning to frown as she stared down at her hand that no longer looked like her own—because there was now a great honking stone plunked down on her ring finger with another band, all heavy diamonds, next to it. It looked ridiculous in and of itself, a finger bedecked and bejeweled like that, given she had the sort of hands that were meant to dig fields rather than loaf about in Italian chapels.

But then the man beside her was turning her to face him, his hands on her shoulders.

Her breath vacated the premises entirely.

His head was descending and she almost felt as if she was dreaming because Lionel Asensio—*Lionel Asensio*—was pressing his mouth to hers.

Everything inside Geraldine simply...stopped.

Innocent Stolen Brides

Married by convenient demand, awakened by passion!

Overlooking the shores of Lake Como, a seemingly perfect high-society wedding is about to take a dramatic and unexpected turn...

As Hope makes her way down the aisle toward her convenient husband-to-be, she finds herself picked up and unceremoniously carried out of the church by a stranger, whose claim on her goes back decades! Once the storm clears, will Hope be able to resist the desert king who stole her away?

Find out in:

The Desert King's Kidnapped Virgin

Being jilted at the altar is an inconvenience Lionel just won't tolerate. So, the commanding billionaire plucks a replacement bride out of the astounded congregation and demands she marry him instead!

Read on in:

The Spaniard's Last-Minute Wife

Both available now!

Caitlin Crews

THE SPANIARD'S LAST-MINUTE WIFE

If you purchased this book without a cover you should be aware that this book is stolen property. It was reported as "unsold and destroyed" to the publisher, and neither the author nor the publisher has received any payment for this "stripped book."

HARLEQUIN®
PRESENTS™

Recycling programs for this product may not exist in your area.

ISBN-13: 978-1-335-59288-0

The Spaniard's Last-Minute Wife

Copyright © 2023 by Caitlin Crews

All rights reserved. No part of this book may be used or reproduced in any manner whatsoever without written permission except in the case of brief quotations embodied in critical articles and reviews.

This is a work of fiction. Names, characters, places and incidents are either the product of the author's imagination or are used fictitiously. Any resemblance to actual persons, living or dead, businesses, companies, events or locales is entirely coincidental.

For questions and comments about the quality of this book, please contact us at CustomerService@Harlequin.com.

Harlequin Enterprises ULC
22 Adelaide St. West, 41st Floor
Toronto, Ontario M5H 4E3, Canada
www.Harlequin.com

Printed in U.S.A.

USA TODAY bestselling, RITA® Award–nominated and critically acclaimed author **Caitlin Crews** has written more than one hundred and thirty books and counting. She has a master's and PhD in English literature, thinks everyone should read more category romance and is always available to discuss her beloved alpha heroes—just ask. She lives in the Pacific Northwest with her comic book–artist husband, is always planning her next trip and will never, ever read all the books in her to-be-read pile. Thank goodness.

Books by Caitlin Crews

Harlequin Presents

Willed to Wed Him
A Secret Heir to Secure His Throne
What Her Sicilian Husband Desires

Innocent Stolen Brides

The Desert King's Kidnapped Virgin

The Outrageous Accardi Brothers

The Christmas He Claimed the Secretary
The Accidental Accardi Heir

The Lost Princess Scandal

Crowning His Lost Princess
Reclaiming His Ruined Princess

Visit the Author Profile page
at Harlequin.com for more titles.

CHAPTER ONE

GERALDINE GERTRUDE CASEY didn't mean to laugh.

Truly, she didn't.

One moment she was sitting with an appropriately poker-faced expression, as suited the occasion, and the next…well. She let out what could only be termed a cackle.

A rather loud cackle, she could admit.

It was involuntary.

Really, it was—though it was also true that she'd had some or other vague notion that she might slip in her objections to the wedding today, assuming that priests here in Italy actually asked if anyone harbored any. Geraldine wasn't certain if they did or didn't and more, harbored no particular certainty that she would understand such a question even if it was asked, as she did not speak Italian.

But another, more salient truth was that she was delirious from flying all the way here on a remarkably uncomfortable overnight flight from Minneapolis via Chicago. She had been crammed into the back of the alarmingly oversize jumbo jet in the middle of a row of tiny, uncomfortable seats with limited recline. Her mother and she had been pressed up against each other from knee to shoulder as they'd passed the unamused baby back and forth between them while pretending that the peace between the two of them wasn't *quite* so precarious in the wake of Geraldine's decision to travel to Italy in the first place.

And while Geraldine and her mother were close, and had always been close, she was fairly sure that the last time she had been that physically close to her mother had been in the womb.

Geraldine had not been all that keen on landing so early in the morning, having slept a total of five minutes, only to have to sort herself out sufficiently to drive her mother and a screaming child from the airport outside Milan all the way to Lake Como, locate the overpriced yet aggressively bland hotel room she'd managed to secure a mere two days before, and then *not* collapse on one of the narrow, monastic beds waiting there. She'd left that to Mama and little Jules, who had been headed into her fifteenth tantrum that morning. Geraldine had changed into a dress, because she was crashing a wedding after all, and had set off to traipse about in the bright heat until she could find her way to this wedding chapel.

What had pleased her was that she'd found it.

Despite the fact there had been no specific information about it anywhere, which had required some next-level sleuthing skills.

Geraldine had expected some kind of security. Quite a lot of security, actually. She had assumed, the groom being the sort of nightmarishly rich billionaire that he was and the bride an heiress in her own right, that she'd be stopped well before she made it to the door of this place and would be required to argue her way inside.

She might even have been looking forward to that argument. A cross she had long been forced to bear—and had thus made it into a weapon—was that no one could ever imagine that a woman who did nothing to enhance her appearance and, in fact, was happy to wear clothing considered "dowdy" so long as it was comfortable, could ever truly be up to no good.

Even if it took a bit of effort to cross the language barrier, Geraldine had been sure that she could brown-hen her way in.

But no brown-henning had been required. There had been only a few people milling about on the narrow road that was really more of a path outside the chapel, looking only vaguely security-like, and none of them had paid her any mind. Perhaps it was because she had a certain way of marching forth, head held high, that went a long way toward convincing anyone who might look that she belonged.

Or perhaps it's actually because you look like

someone's maiden aunt, she told herself dryly. *Emphasis on maiden and aunt.*

Then again, she did that on purpose. What wasn't on purpose was the fact that she'd made a bit of a racket coming inside the ancient building. Also, the Italian breeze had caught the door behind her, wrenched it from her grip, and slammed it shut.

Loudly.

But what Geraldine had noticed immediately wasn't who was or was not glaring at her for causing a commotion. Instead, she was quite surprised to find that the bride was not only walking herself down the aisle, she was already about halfway done with the entire exercise.

And though the bride had stopped and looked back over her shoulder, all dressed in white and eyes solemn, Geraldine hadn't seized the moment the way she should have.

The bride turned around again and had started for the altar once more.

Leaving Geraldine to slink into the last pew much more quietly than she'd entered, her mind racing.

She had shoved her glasses up her nose as she'd sat, a nervous habit she preferred to deny she possessed. Usually she wore her contacts, but she'd been sure they would dry out her eyes on that flight and she hadn't had time to pop them back in while changing in that tiny hotel room, her mother muttering *I told you so* beneath her breath and little Jules in mid-tantrum.

And your contact lenses have nothing to do with anything, she had snapped at herself.

She'd reminded herself then, rather severely, that it wouldn't do her any good to have come all this way if she wasn't prepared to jump in as planned at any given opportunity.

Like the one she'd squandered just then.

And so she had been drumming up her courage to leap to her feet and stop the proceedings—and she'd required that courage not because she was in any doubt that her cause was just, and certainly not because she was any sort of shy or retiring mouse, but because she was Midwestern born and bred and, deep within her, had an inbred horror of causing a scene of any kind no matter the reason—when the door to the chapel had slammed wide open again.

Louder this time.

And as it did, a ferocious-looking man came striding in, dressed in black and seeming also to *exude* a matching black fury as he came.

He did not take the first available seat, as Geraldine had.

Instead, he'd helped himself to the bride.

He'd found her in the aisle, tossed her over his shoulder without a word, and then strode right on out again.

And Geraldine had always taken pride in her practical, rational nature—so much so that she even dressed so that said nature was what was noticed about her, first and foremost. She was a woman who had always enjoyed the company of facts and the books where those facts were so often housed. The cool, leather-bound intellect of a library was the happiest place she could imagine, and she would be back in hers right now if it weren't for poor motherless baby Jules.

But she couldn't claim that she was thinking about Jules after the door slammed shut behind the man and the kidnapped bride, leaving the few people left in this chapel to stare at each other blankly.

Maybe she wasn't thinking at all.

Because she let out that cackle. And once she'd laughed, she hadn't seen any particularly compelling reason to *stop* laughing.

Geraldine was still laughing, in fact.

With a little more sleep, or really *any* sleep, she was certain she might have controlled herself—because didn't she always control herself?—but then again, perhaps she wouldn't have bothered.

Because it was a certain kind of funny, wasn't it? She had pulled together a shocking amount of money to come all this way to stop a wedding that hadn't needed stopping after all.

If only someone had thought to mention that the bride would be abducted before the vows were spoken, Geraldine thought, and set herself off again.

She was rummaging around in her bag for the tissues she always kept close to hand—because her eyes were watering the more she laughed, another likely consequence of that endless flight—and she was making that cackling sound again, which only made her laugh more. But eventually she found a tissue. She dabbed at her eyes, like the sort of lady who didn't go around hooting and hollering at the abortive wedding ceremonies of total strangers.

Only after she'd calmed herself slightly did she become aware of a kind of shadow that fell over her. A strange sort of shadow that made every last cell in her entire body seem to tighten of its own accord.

Only then did she look up.

And up.

And still farther up.

To find the would-be groom standing above her, a thunderous look upon his face.

This close to him, Geraldine made the entirely unwelcome discovery that he was significantly more attractive in person than she had imagined.

She had researched this man exhaustively. She had therefore spent a lot of time imagining not only him, but what she would do and say should she encounter him as she'd planned to do. She had any number of lectures in her back pocket, but the sight of him in real life was…

Unexpected, somehow.

And he was *glowering* at her.

The *he* in question was Lionel Asensio, born to a revolting amount of wealth in Spain somewhere. He was the result of generations of affluence, the very notion of which sent a bolt of dismay straight to Geraldine's deeply understated Midwestern soul.

Lionel himself had come of age more serious by far than the family playboys and international Lotharios who had preceded him. He had spent rather longer in educational pursuits than at least the three previous generations had done. He'd gotten a double first at Cambridge, no easy task, no matter how well-connected the student. And it was with a coveted graduate degree in business from Harvard that he had marched, grim-faced if the pictures were any indication, into the sad little family business that was likely no more than a tax shelter and turned it into a vibrant multinational corporation that some spectators claimed must have tripled his inherited wealth within ten years.

In other words, he was mind-numbingly, incomprehensibly wealthy, and yet that was not her objection to him.

It was not even his excess of male beauty, which she had expected to be harsh and off-putting. Every picture she'd seen of him had featured him glowering about just as he was now, either at the people he was with or straight into the camera itself.

She'd thought he looked surprisingly pugilistic, if not downright mean, for a man who could have no battles to fight.

It was true, she saw. He still did.

But in person there was a magnetism to this man that no picture could possibly convey. She felt her whole body shiver into a shock of awareness, as if she had no choice but to sit up straighter. As if the force of his regard commanded her flesh to respond.

Worse, it seemed primed to do his bidding.

Geraldine had always taken pride in her height, inherited from any number of her possibly Viking ancestresses, because she enjoyed that she stood taller than many women in her bare feet.

But the way this man looked down at her, she felt tiny. Somehow *delightfully* fragile. As if he could snap her in two with no effort whatsoever and more alarming, that she might like that. Or better still, tuck her away in one of his pockets.

She had the stray, treacherous thought that he could not possibly be the man she thought he was because there was something deep in her own bones that told her otherwise, that *knew better*—

But it didn't matter what *her bones* said, she told herself sharply. What mattered was what her poor, lost cousin Seanna had told her before she died—that there had been only one name she had ever uttered. And that Geraldine had come all the way to Italy to make certain that there would be justice for her cousin and her cousin's daughter, one way or another.

Even if it meant going toe-to-toe with a man who made her *want* to quiver.

To *quiver*, of all things.

He rattled off some sort of dark demand in what she thought was Italian, given where they were, though it may well have been Spanish for all she understood either language. And she meant to reply, she really did, but Geraldine's body did not seem to be interested in obeying her commands.

It was him.

It was the way he *looked* at her. He was dressed in his fine and elegant clothes that should have made him look fussy, but did not. Instead, it was as if they couldn't quite contain him. As if this chapel itself was too small.

As if he carried a brooding force within him, rough and sensual, that her body recognized instinctively.

Whatever the reason, she couldn't say a word.

"Let me guess, you speak only English," he said in the face of her ongoing silence, in a voice that seemed to cut straight into her, sounding both faintly British and undoubtedly Spanish at once.

And also dripping with disdain.

"I have conversational French and can read German," Geraldine retorted, stung by the disdain and the inference that she was one of *those people*, forever barging around the world, expecting everyone to speak her language. She'd read all about them. *She* would never be so conceited. "I'm also working on my Japanese. Since you asked."

"Perhaps you will share, then—in any of those languages—what it is you find so amusing."

"Humor is very subjective," she demurred, spurred by a sudden sense of self-preservation she wasn't sure she had ever felt before. It had something to do with his eyes, the color of coffee too bitter to drink. It was something about all the harshly elegant lines of his face, like old sculptures that had never been meant for the menial gaze of the peasants. It was that last notion that infuriated her enough to keep talking. "I doubt you would find it as funny as I do. What with all the cultural differences and whatnot."

"Try me."

It was not request.

And Geraldine found that she had to remind herself, sharply, that she was not here for this man's entertainment. She was not here for him to command her in any way.

She was not here for *him* at all. This was about Seanna. This was about the daughter her cousin had left behind.

Despite her body's worrying reactions to Lionel Asensio in all his considerable state, she forced herself to get to her feet. Right then, to *prove* she was unaffected.

But she found that it had not been a trick of the Italian pew where she'd been sitting. It was no optical illusion. Lionel Asensio really did tower over her.

Even when she was standing tall.

"It's not every day that you see a bride carried off from a groom who does not seem to mind a bit," she pointed out.

As she stood there in her ill-fitting dress in this Italian chapel filled with incense and sunlight and this glowering, appallingly handsome man.

Not *quite* quivering.

And really, Geraldine had just thrown that last bit out there to be provoking. But as she said it, she could see that it was true. For one thing, the man was standing here, talking to her about jokes and languages. He wasn't racing out of the chapel himself. He wasn't ordering the people around him, all his minions if she had to guess by their deferential expressions, to chase after his bride for him. Neither he nor they were calling in the authorities.

"Who are you?" he asked her, instead of addressing what she would have assumed was the more glaring issue of his missing bride.

Yet it did not occur to her to disobey him by not answering the question. "My name is Geraldine Gertrude Casey, not that I expect that to mean anything to you."

He did not quite incline his head. Though there was what appeared to be an infinitesimal gesture in that direction. Almost. "It does not."

And then he infuriated her all the more by subjecting her to what could only be called an overtly thorough head-to-toe *examination* that was in no possible way appropriate, much less polite. That too-dark, too-intense gaze of his traveled from the top of her admittedly frazzled head all the way down to her sturdy travel shoes, then made its slow way up again, taking care to linger over her deliberately frumpy dress.

It was *deliberate,* she reminded herself as the urge

to flush in some kind of heretofore unknown embarrassment nearly took her over. *If you cared in the slightest about how dresses look upon your frame, you would have bought one that fit it.*

She then told herself that when she did flush, and all over, it was from fury.

Geraldine was well used to not exactly bewitching men with her charms. Though she had many gifts in this life, and was proud of all of them, that particular skill had never been one of them. It had been her poor cousin who had possessed that talent, and nothing in Seanna's short and largely troubled life had convinced Geraldine that she ought to think she'd missed out. She didn't.

But it had also been a long while, possibly since she'd been in those dreadful middle school years, since anyone had dared look at her the way this man did now.

As if he was sizing her up and finding her wanting—*as a woman*, clearly—in every possible way.

It almost made her laugh all over again.

She was certain that mad heat bubbling up within her was *laughter*.

"You do not look married," he said, and there was a note in that silk-and-steel voice of his that she could not say she liked.

The insinuation was all too obvious. He did not have to ask, *Who would marry the likes of you?*— and yet the question hung over the old stone floor as if it was smokier by far than the burning incense.

It got right up her nose.

Normally she would have found hilarious the very idea that some hulking billionaire found a librarian from Minnesota not to his taste.

I should hope not, she might have said with a peal of laughter. *Or I would assume I'd lived the whole of my life entirely wrong.*

But today Geraldine was overly tired. So tired she felt pale straight through. And she did not like being looked at and analyzed with so much *derision*, as if she was a bit of spoiled produce in a bargain bin set out in front of the sort of down-market grocery store that she, personally, did not frequent.

"I cannot imagine what it is you think *married* looks like," she shot back at him, a bit recklessly. Maybe more than *a bit*, given that she was on her own here in this chapel while *he* had brought a selection of minions with him. "Though I would imagine that anyone married to *you* would likely look desperate for escape. If your previous almost-bride is any indication."

"I will take that as a no, you are not married," he replied, with a certain languid note in that voice of his that was even more insulting. *Because how could you be?* was the next question that he didn't actually need to put into words for it to hang there between them.

Smoky and rude.

"I'm not sure that's the issue I would be harping on if I was in your shoes," she retorted. "I'm pretty sure we saw *your* bride fail entirely to put up any kind of fight at all while being carried away from you and this wedding, friend."

And she thought she saw a flicker of *something* in his dark gaze at that. But before she could press him any further, or dig her own grave any deeper, more like, he silenced her simply enough—by placing his hand on her upper arm and thereby urging her to walk with him back up the aisle.

Ushering her along as if she was the one being forcibly removed from the premises, with exactly as little actual *force* as the previous bride had experienced on her way out.

Only they were headed in the opposite direction, not that she had it in her to care too much about that.

It was that hand, Geraldine told herself through the strange haze that descended. It was *his* hand, or more precisely, that she could feel the wild heat of it. Not only where it gripped her upper arm, but all through her body.

As if the hold he had on her was nothing more than an ignition point, and everything else was ablaze.

She could feel the flames dance through her, licking this way and that along her arms and then all through the rest of her, finding every secret part of her body and setting it alight. One after the next, as if every step she took was from one bonfire to the next.

Her breasts felt heavy. And deep between her legs, something began to ache.

Then, before she knew it, Geraldine was standing at the head of the chapel's surprisingly long aisle, staring at the priest who stood there—though she couldn't seem to make sense of anything.

Not the priest as he began to speak in what she was certain was Italian this time. Not the rumbling sounds that seemed to come as much from the man beside her as *through her,* too, as if he was nothing short of an earthquake.

Except she was so *hot* when she had always imagined that, should she find herself confronted with the earth itself heaving about beneath her feet, she would be cold to the core, iced over with fear.

There were words exchanged, which she could understand even if she didn't speak the language. And she was certain she *tried* to object, but she couldn't seem to make her mouth—or any other part of herself—act properly.

Especially when Lionel Asensio, that impossible creature, turned to face her and while he did, pulled her hands into his.

Then held them there while out of the corners of her eyes, the chapel seemed to spin a little drunkenly.

Geraldine tried not to pay attention, which was her usual policy with actual drunks, too.

That was just as well, because all she really *could* manage to do was gaze stupidly at him, because his hands were on hers and she couldn't seem to *breathe,* while he spoke rapidly. Almost carelessly, she might have thought, except the look in his eyes was intense.

Particularly when he slid two rings onto her finger, one after the next, then gazed at her when the priest spoke in his turn.

"You must reply," Lionel said gravely, in English when the priest was finished. And the silence seemed to billow between them like still more smoke.

"But I…" she began. Her tongue felt too large. Her jaw too small. "I really don't…"

"All you must say is *yes*," he told her, again in that deeply serious manner.

And then, as she stared at him, fire dancing where it liked inside of her, one of his dark brows rose.

As if he was daring her.

And Geraldine was not a *daring* sort of person. The only thing she had done in the whole of her life that could be described as anything approaching *daring* was the fact that she'd come here, determined to make this very man take responsibility for what he'd done to her cousin.

Surely that alone should have had her stepping back and shaking her hands free of his, reclaiming herself from…whatever spell this was.

But his eyes were bittersweet chocolate, dark and rich. He gleamed like gold, though he was in no way blond. As if he, himself, was liquid gold from within. And that dark, aristocratic eyebrow felt like a call to arms.

She did not have it in her to do anything but whisper, *"yes."*

Like the obedient soul she had always, secretly, imagined she was not.

And then everything seemed to speed up again. The priest was going on in Italian, Lionel was responding. Geraldine was beginning to frown as she stared down at her hand that no longer looked like her own—because there was now a great honking stone plunked down on her ring finger with another band, all heavy diamonds, next to it. It looked ridiculous in and of itself, a finger bedecked and bejeweled like that, given she had the sort of hands that were meant to dig fields rather than loaf about in Italian chapels.

But then the man beside her was turning her to face him, his hands on her shoulders.

Her breath vacated the premises entirely.

Because his head was descending and she almost felt as if she was dreaming, because Lionel Asensio—*Lionel Asensio*—was pressing his mouth to hers.

Everything inside Geraldine simply…stopped.

His lips were warm, and stern.

They pressed against hers in unmistakable command.

And everything that Geraldine was or ever had been disappeared, melting away in the face of a roaring fire unlike any she had ever known.

It was too bright.

It was too *hot*.

It was all too—

Everything spun around and around, and not just in her peripheral vision.

A strange sort of languor melded with the heat, invading her limbs, making her hotter by the second.

And she was so tired and it must have been the jet lag and there was too much incense everywhere and surely she hadn't married this preposterously dark creature, so demanding and daring and—

But then everything went mercifully blank.

CHAPTER TWO

LIONEL ASENSIO WAS well used to causing a commotion in the female population, whenever and however he encountered them. His staff liked to whisper, where they imagined he could not hear them, that he could barely walk down a street without women clinging to his every limb.

That was an exaggeration.

But not much of an exaggeration.

And yet despite all that, he was quite certain that he had never made a woman *faint* before.

Then again, he had never married one, either.

It was hard not to conclude that the two were somehow related.

He caught her, of course. Like it or not, the tryingly named *Geraldine Gertrude Casey* was his wife now, and Lionel hoped he was not the kind of man who let a woman under his protection crash to the ground no matter the circumstances.

Today was not the day to change the whole of his character, despite the fact he had gone ahead and changed his life over the course of a short ceremony. No matter that he intended there to be precious few ramifications from that decision, there would be *some*, and yet he had still done it.

He caught her long before she hit the floor. He swept her up into his arms, lifting his chin at his assistant in the first pew as he turned. The man leaped to his feet and headed for the door at once, and Lionel knew that meant that his car would be brought around so that, hopefully, he could leave this place without the ever-lurking paparazzi any the wiser that he been here in the first place. Much less that he had gone ahead and gotten married to a literal nonentity, as far as he could tell at a glance. Not to mention that said nonentity had been so overset with sheer joy at the sudden dramatic shift in her circumstances that she had literally swooned in his arms.

Something in him chose to remind him that it had not been *joy* he had seen all over the woman's face, but he pushed that aside. Because it should have been joy. She should have been prostrate with gratitude.

Perhaps this was her version of precisely that.

His second assistant approached. "I will need to know who this woman is, obviously," Lionel said, keeping his voice low in case anyone not in his employ was lurking about in the shadows. "I will need to know everything she has eaten for breakfast over the past ten years, at a minimum, and anything else you can turn up. She said her name was *Geraldine Gertrude Casey*, of all things, and I cannot think why an American tourist should turn up in the middle of a private ceremony the way she did, then laugh with so little attempt to conceal it when the wedding ended so precipitously. Find out why, please."

His second assistant nodded, then stepped back, typing away on her device.

He ordered his third and fourth assistants to assemble his legal team, for there would need to be contracts drawn up, replacing the name of the Cartwright heiress with Geraldine's. There might also have to be some creativity involved in the documents for today's events, but he had discovered that there was precious little in the world that could not be altered to suit him. All it took was money. And as he considered the woman he had almost married, he beckoned yet another assistant close.

"We will need to ascertain what has become of the previous bride, please. And whether she requires assistance." He felt a slight pang at that, but Hope Cartwright had known exactly what he was about. And that he had needed a bride today, come hell or high water. As theirs had been an entirely cold-blooded business venture that had never trafficked in or near any emotional terrain, Lionel assumed that his near-wife would understand that he could not do anything but what he had done here, not that he intended to consult her about it. But that didn't mean he couldn't put his men on the case to determine what had actually happened to her today.

It is literally the least you can do, came a voice

inside that sounded suspiciously like the conscience his grandmother had been at such pains to instill in him all his life.

Only when all of these instructions had been fired off left and right and his people were hurrying about with tasks to perform did Lionel finally take a moment to look down at the woman he had held in his arms all the while.

His initial impression of her was that she was, decidedly, what he knew was called a *frump*. Dowdy almost beyond comprehension. He had seen her when she'd come in, thanks to the racket she'd made, and had wondered in passing what dreary organization had set its church mouse free to crash weddings in Italy.

But then she had laughed when no one else in the chapel had dared.

When everyone else had been frozen into place, and silent, awaiting his reaction.

And then on top of this she had been, if not openly defiant, markedly and noticeably unimpressed with Lionel himself.

He was…not used to such reactions.

Not unless said reactions were themselves a bit of playacting by those hoping to differentiate themselves from the crowd, but that was not the impression he'd gotten from this woman.

Something had shifted again when she'd stood and proved herself not to be a tiny, frail little thing. She was tall enough, not an unusual circumstance in his circles, but she was not a whittled-down figurine all gaunt bones in the vague shape of a woman. She was not emaciated—fashionably or otherwise—as so many women were these days, as if starving themselves was a bit of sport and they wanted a medal.

He would have said instead that she looked…well. Tired and frumpy, certainly, but there was a smoothness to her shape. A pleasing hint of an actual figure, somewhere beneath that tent-like monstrosity of a dress.

Now she was in his arms, her eyes closed behind the unduly large glasses she wore. Shut, her eyelids covered the unusual green of her gaze and the way she'd stared at him so owlishly, with that intensity of regard that had called him to a kind of attention he did not quite understand.

Lionel did not wish to understand it. He dismissed the notion that he should. Because this close, he was aware of a great many things about the woman he'd just married.

Whether he wanted to be aware of her or not.

Her skin was extraordinary. She seemed to *glow*, somehow, and not simply because the flush he'd seen all over her earlier had left some marks. Lionel would have said that no woman alive in these greedy and calculated times still blushed, but this one had proved him wrong.

Yet now the deepness of that flush had receded like the tide and all he could see was softness and that impossible *glow*.

Her hair was dark and was twisted back in one of those hideous claw devices that looked like nothing so much as the return of the Inquisition to him, and not in a manner he would ever dream of calling *artful*. Lionel felt certain that she had thrown it back to get it out of her way and had likely thought no more about it.

He could not account for why he could not seem to do the same. It had something to do with the fact that he could smell the shampoo she'd used, a bright pop of coconut and papaya, of all things. She smelled of the fruity, frothy cocktails he would never drink and there was no reason at all he should find that appealing.

Particularly when she was clad from neck to ankles in her entirely shapeless dress that appeared to be covered in some kind of indefinable floral element. The hint of flowers, though their shape gave him no clue what precisely they were supposed to be. The garment made her look like nothing so much as a rather dreadful couch.

Yet the woman in his arms was not shapeless. He could feel it. She was soft and warm and worse by far, he could feel her curves.

Lionel did not wish to feel anything. His father and his grandfather before him had been men of great passion, by their reckoning and according to their excuses. Lionel thought of them as men made of greed, for anything that caught their fancy. Or any passing whim. They had been heedless, reckless in every respect, and had waved it all away by claiming that it was their enormity of feeling that made them act as they did. That they could not be expected to rein themselves in, for they were men of great appetites and needed to feed.

To Lionel, the pair of them had been nothing but vampires. He had vowed that he would never let his feelings dictate his behavior in that way.

Or in any way.

His grandmother had taken a similarly dim view of the man she had married and the one she had raised, and it was her influence that had saved him from following in their footsteps.

He was grateful to his *abuelita* every day.

And yet this woman in his arms smelled like the tropics while looking like a library.

Lionel knew he had never kissed a mouth as plain as Geraldine's. He could not account for why the experience still reverberated through him, as if this woman was a fault line, and having tripped over her, everything was now far more precarious.

He was Lionel Asensio. He did not *do* precarious.

But none of that mattered, because the deed was done. She had married him, not that he had allowed him any doubt that she might balk once he had decided that she might as well take the Cartwright heiress's place. And Lionel was not one to spend too much time looking backward. There was nothing to be done now but to move on.

Into what came next.

He was already steeling himself for it.

Lionel carried her from the chapel, already working out what his next steps would need to be, when he felt the woman, his *wife*, stir in his arms. He paused on the steps outside, looking down at her as those surprisingly dark lashes moved against the bright skin of her face.

He had no idea why he found the sight so captivating.

And then, once more, he found himself pinned by that solemn green regard.

He expected her to react badly and braced himself, but though he could feel a new tension invade her form, she only held his gaze. She blinked.

Once.

"Why are you carrying me?" she asked, very calmly. And quite reasonably enough, to his mind.

"You were overcome," he told her with the matter-of-factness he was known for. "Had I had not caught you, you would have fainted dead away on the ancient stones and would no doubt have a bruised head besides. You may consider this my first gift to you as your husband."

Another long, slow blink that somehow seemed to roll through her. All through her body, so that even the ghastly shoes she wore seemed a part of it, and then it all seemed to roll through him, too. Lionel could not imagine why he felt the urge to stand taller.

"Impossible," she said in that same calm, collected manner. And now the way she was looking at him seemed to brand him a liar, of all things. "I have never fainted in my life."

"Then I congratulate you, Geraldine." And that odd name felt like one of those silly drinks in his mouth. "For it seems today is a day of a great many firsts for you."

He was certain that what he saw ignite in her gaze then was temper. Lionel did not do temper, and so he set her down on her feet. And pretended not to notice when she shook off the hand he kept on her, to make sure she remained steady.

"I don't know what happened," she told him, in that same brisk manner that also seemed to suggest that she thought he was at fault nonetheless. "But I can assure you, I do not make a habit of *losing consciousness* at the slightest provocation."

"Perhaps, for you, the provocation was not so slight." He lifted his shoulder when her brows drew together. "Have you ever been kissed before?"

The frown she gave him then was ferocious. "What kind of question is *that*?"

"I will tell you," he continued, fully aware that the way she'd answered him was a confession all its own, "that I suspect you never have."

"You are mistaken." Her voice was frosty.

"Your reactions suggest otherwise." He eyed her. "Among other things."

Her eyes blazed. "I am devastated that you find me so lacking in so many areas. No one else has ever complained."

"Somehow, that does not surprise me," Lionel said, which was true. As he doubted there was anyone *to* complain.

But when his car pulled up in front of the chapel, he ushered her down the steps and she walked along with him gamely enough. He was intrigued, despite himself, that for all the many ways she seemed determined to defy him, all he needed to do was put his hand on her and she would follow him wherever he liked.

Or perhaps *intrigued* was not the right word.

This time they were both sitting in the back seat of the car and driving away from the chapel before she seemed able to collect herself and look around.

Or collect herself as much as a woman could while her face had come over red again.

Another blush when he had thought one odd enough.

Remarkable, he found himself thinking. When the only remarkable part of any of this was the lengths that he, Lionel Asensio, who was feared and admired the world over, should go to please his grandmother.

"I am staying in a hotel," Geraldine told him. Rather crossly. "And I don't think it is in this direction."

"Only tell me which hotel it is and I will have my men gather your things and cancel your reservation," he said, and he thought he sounded rather magnanimous, all things considered.

He did not expect her to glare at him the way she did. "Why would I do that?"

Lionel stopped worrying about how he was going to sort out the mess this wedding had become and focused on her. "Perhaps your fainting spell has made you confused."

"I don't think I'm the only one in that position," Geraldine replied, in a tart sort of way that did not sound as if *confusion* was much of a concern here. He told himself he was grateful. He should have been grateful. "In case you've already forgotten, you had a very different bride walking down the aisle toward you not long ago. You're supposed to be married to an entirely different woman. And I'm not sure that you're actually married to me. I wasn't in my right mind. Clearly."

He could not say that he cared for the way she said that last word.

"The priest asked you to state your vows and you did." Lionel let his mouth curve in what was likely not much of a smile, given the way she looked at him. "I am afraid it is done now. We are married whether either one of us likes it or not."

"None of this makes sense." She shook her head, looking out the car window and then back at him. "You're not even Italian."

This was the most reasonable thing she'd said so far. Or at least the most familiar thing. "You seem very certain. Almost as if you know who I am. I am flattered."

"You're a famously rich man," Geraldine said flatly, which was not the way people normally referred to his consequence or position. "I'm sure people recognize you all the time."

"I will tell you now that I do not much care if they do or do not," Lionel told her, honestly. "So if that was the reason you came to the chapel today, I suspect you will find the next few years of your life a great trial."

She only glared at him. "But what I don't understand is why you, a Spanish billionaire, were marrying an Englishwoman here, in Italy."

"Perhaps, in addition to never having been kissed, you are also unfamiliar with the concept of a destination wedding," Lionel suggested. When her eyes flashed anew, he had the wholly uncharacteristic urge to laugh. When he prided himself on his stern and sober steadiness, in all things.

He had no idea what it was about this woman, who was unlike any other woman he had ever been linked to in any way, that made him feel so unlike himself.

If he could have, he would have let her out of the car and never thought of her again. But that was not possible now.

"You are quite right," Geraldine said, her voice so sardonic that it should have left marks. There was a part of him that wanted to check. "I have never heard of such a thing as a destination wedding. And obviously, because I wear glasses, I am untouched. Entirely. Your perception is truly astounding."

But he could tell that she was lying about the *untouched* part. It was the way she lapsed off into the ether every time he touched her. It was the way she flushed so charmingly, then seemed to go off into some kind of a daze.

And it was the fact that she had brought it up again.

As if the notion that he had thought such a thing of her stung her, and why should it if it was untrue? If someone suggested to Lionel that *he* was untouched, he thought he really would laugh.

And so Lionel did not choose to tell her what he could so easily discern. Just as he did not tell her that this wedding had taken place here in Italy because it was the sort of place his grandmother might believe he would choose to get married without it being close enough to the family estates in Andalusia that she might feel moved to attend. So when he presented her with the bride—the very bride she had been demanding for years now—he could explain precisely why she had not been invited to attend at all.

I was thinking only of your comfort, Abuelita, he would assure her.

His grandmother would not believe him, of course, but that was another day's problem.

He pushed those things away and settled back in his seat. His phone was in his pocket and he checked it, reading the message his man had sent him.

Bride number one boarded a helicopter with her abductor. Under her own steam and with no apparent distress. There did not appear to be any force applied.

Lionel tucked the phone away again. If Hope Cartwright had found herself a better option, who was he to complain? No contracts had been signed. Hope and he had come to an agreement, but all signatures had been saved for after the ceremony, when the both of them had taken the final step.

He had fully expected that Hope Cartwright would make him a perfectly fine wife.

But he could admit, sitting in the car while Geraldine Casey gazed at him with her green eyes nothing short of baleful, that he had never found the Cartwright heiress's company even remotely so interesting.

He was not at all sure what that might say about him.

"Where you taking me?" Geraldine asked, and now that he had returned his phone to his pocket, and was no longer standing in a wedding ceremony without a bride, he took his time studying her. He had no idea why a woman would drape herself in the sort of garment she wore, but it did nothing to hide the shockingly elegant line of her neck or the hollow there, where he could see her pulse fluttering.

As if he interested her too, loathe as she seemed to be to admit it.

Though he acknowledged there was a possible other reason. "I do not wish to do you any harm, if that is what you mean."

"You married a perfect stranger who you happened to find in the back of a wedding chapel," Geraldine pointed out and this time, she sounded somewhat less calm. "And not just any stranger. *I* don't like you."

"Impossible," he said, much the way she'd said it before. "All women like me. Or, I should say, I have never met one who does not."

Geraldine sat very straight beside him. She turned her body in the bucket seat so that she could look at him fully, and took her time pushing her glasses up the length of her nose. Making certain to broadcast her disapproval all the while.

"I know you to be the worst kind of man," she said, very distinctly, and kept her gaze trained on him while she said it. "A monster in every respect."

And it should not have mattered in the least what a woman he did not know, a woman he had not exactly thought highly of in the mere hour of their acquaintance, thought of him. It should not have mattered, yet Lionel found he did not care for the way she said that.

And he cared even less for *how little* he liked it.

Especially when she continued. "You hide behind this notion that you are somehow a creature of propriety," she told him in that same stern, certain manner that felt a great deal like a ringing conviction.

"When the truth is, you are at least as licentious as anyone else. And a great deal more than some."

And Lionel found that he could not be offended at such an absurdity. It was exactly as he'd imagined he might react if she'd gone the other way and proclaimed he was a virgin. Laughable and little else—except, perhaps, intrigued about how she had managed to come to such an odd conclusion about his character.

It hardly seemed to matter that it was completely and utterly false. That was how ludicrous it was.

"I will give you this, Geraldine," he said, and he sounded as close to laughter as he had in some while. He couldn't remember the last time he'd strayed into the vicinity. "I have never before been accused of such a thing. Rather its opposite."

"It says nothing about a person when they only interact with those who are as powerful as they are," Geraldine said in that same way, as if she was laying out evidence before him and all of it led to his guilt. It was nothing short of extraordinary. "What matters is how a person with power treats someone who has none. What matters is preying upon a vulnerable woman, convincing her that it is the deepest sort of love only to abandon her when she's pregnant."

"I beg your pardon." Lionel frowned at her. "Are you suggesting that I got a girl pregnant and cast her aside?"

Geraldine's green gaze was direct. "I know you did."

And he did not understand why there was a part

of him that wanted to argue. And more, wanted to make her take back such lies against him when he should not care—when were there not rumors and lies circulating about him? It came with his name and the way he'd chosen to live his life.

Instead, Lionel sighed. "That is ridiculous for any number of reasons, but let me tell you the foremost reason. You know who I am. You know that I have tremendous wealth and power at my fingertips. What do you imagine could compel me to marry like this?" When Geraldine didn't answer, he continued, impatiently. "So quickly, almost furtively, and to a woman I do not know at all. What could account for such a thing?"

She blinked, but her gaze did not become any less baleful. "Rich men are very strange. It is one of their most well-known characteristics, though we are all encouraged to consider it *eccentricity* and nothing more."

"My father and my grandfather before him were sometimes entertaining at a party, but were otherwise largely useless," Lionel told her, and restrained himself from asking if she had as many *rich men* in her life as she did lovers. "This is not a matter of opinion, so much as it is inarguable fact. The only family I have left, and the only one worth a damn, is my grandmother. And she wants nothing more than a grandchild."

"I'm sure you think that makes you relatable," Geraldine began hotly, "but I don't really see why—"

"It is statistically improbable that I could impregnate a woman with the precautions I always take," he interrupted her, "but not impossible. What *is* impossible is that a woman might tell me that she carried my child, prove this to be true, and then watch me walk away from her. This would never happen. It never did happen."

"But it did," she insisted.

"On the contrary, Geraldine," he said, and there was something about her name. Something about the taste of it—but he kept his attention on that grave green gaze of hers. "I would rejoice. My grandmother's dearest wish would be fulfilled at last and with ease. I would marry any girl who was pregnant with my child, sing a round of hosannas, and call it a day."

Geraldine only stared back at him, frowning, and not as if she thought she was confused. It was clear that she thought he was.

"That's not at all what happened." And she leaned in closer then, so he could see that there was not one part of her that did not believe what she was telling him. She was totally and completely sure that she was speaking the truth—he could see that all over her as easily as he'd seen her blush. "My cousin died in childbirth. Alone and with your name in her mouth."

"I cannot account for that," Lionel told her in the same grave manner. "But the child cannot be mine."

"I have the baby with me," Geraldine said, ignoring him. Another thing that did not usually happen to him in the presence of women. Or anyone else. "Her name is Jules, she is wonderful, and I intend to make certain you take responsibility for her at last, Lionel. Whether I am married to you or not."

CHAPTER THREE

GERALDINE WAS PROUD of the ringing tones she used then and the way her voice filled the car, as if there was no difference whatsoever in their positions. As if she commanded the same authority he did—because she did, back home in her library.

And also because, she kept telling herself with what might possibly be some small bit of desperation, there were no differences between them that she did not allow. He had more money and more unearned power because of it, certainly, but otherwise she need not feel the least bit cowed by this man unless she *wished* to feel cowed, which she did not.

Of course, there was also the confusing part where she'd accidentally *married* the man in what could not possibly have been a real ceremony—though that priest had certainly seemed real enough—

I refuse to be cowed by anyone, Geraldine told herself stoutly, cutting off that unhelpful line of internal wittering. *Especially a man who treated poor Seanna so shabbily.*

She did not like the voice inside that suggested that, perhaps, the person who had treated Seanna the shabbiest might well have been Seanna.

Geraldine told herself, as she always did, that thinking such a thing was unfair. Seanna had been young and impressionable. It hadn't been her fault that she'd been too naive to see what was happening to her until it was too late. Or if it had been, well, there were others far *more* at fault.

Like this man.

Lionel Asensio, who had treated her cousin the way he had and who Geraldine had somehow let *kiss* her—and even if it was a part of that so-called wedding ceremony, there was no excuse.

Lionel Asensio, who looked wholly unscathed to Geraldine's eye, which was an injustice in one profoundly male form.

Lionel Asensio, who was looking at her now as if she'd sprouted an extra head when she'd fainted.

Not that Geraldine could get her head around *that*, either. She was no wilting flower. She had never *swooned* before.

She was sure that was his fault, too. Somehow.

And she was certainly not planning to dwell on the way it had felt to come awake in his arms, warm against his chest, as if the whole of the world and all she would ever be or want to be was…him. That harsh, aristocratic face, tipped toward hers. That gleam in his dark gaze, as if he could and would hold her forever.

As if he really was her husband.

She'd had the strange and yet comforting notion that, at last, she was precisely where she belonged.

Odious thought, she told herself now. *You must have hit your head, despite what he told you. There will no doubt be a bump to make sense of all this later.*

As for right now, she told herself she was *sitting in her power.* She had made it perfectly clear that she meant what she said and whether he believed it or not, Geraldine was prepared to do whatever was necessary to make sure that Jules was taken care of as she deserved. As Seanna had deserved, too. The confusion of this strangest of days was nothing compared with her mission here.

And she felt something inside her ease, almost, because she was finally doing the thing she'd promised Seanna she would. Again and again in those last days, when she hadn't known if her cousin could even hear her any longer.

"I can see that you have nothing to say for yourself," she said a few moments later, when all Lionel did was gaze back at her with that faintly bemused expression on his supremely arrogant face. "I'm not surprised. I know it is often difficult to face the consequences of one's actions."

Or so she had heard and witnessed. *She* had personally never left anyone pregnant by the side of the metaphoric road, so *she* was not an expert on these matters. Only their terribly sad and unjust consequences.

Which, apparently, Lionel Asensio had avoided until now. It had astonished Geraldine that no matter how deep her digging on him had gone, she had found no other illegitimate children knocking about. When she'd expected to find several battalions' worth, at the least.

"Mi querida esposa," he murmured, seeming to *expand* somehow, there in the back seat of the car as it bumped its way along ancient Italian roads she might have found beautiful at any other time. To say nothing of that famously beautiful lake gleaming in the distance. "My dear wife, you seem to have me confused with someone else."

"I know exactly who you are," Geraldine told him, and shoved her glasses back up her nose. Perhaps more vigorously than necessary. "Yours is the name my cousin spoke again and again on her deathbed. And just to be certain, I spent months researching you after she passed."

"I do not doubt these things, necessarily," he said, though there was a certain sheen in his dark-coffee gaze that made her suspect that he did, in fact, harbor more than a little doubt. But if so, it did not appear to upset him overmuch. All he did was relax back into the seat, managing to look somehow indolent and stern at once. Geraldine had no earthly idea why a simple shift of his body should seem to run straight through her like something electric. She assured itself it was further evidence of his guilt. "However, a few words from a woman in some distress—no matter her circumstances—and whatever it is you call research do not add up to proof, I am afraid. That would require blood tests."

The *audacity*. Geraldine bristled. "I'm not at all surprised you have found a way to excuse yourself. Isn't that just like a man? Always willing to shirk responsibility at the faintest indication—"

"I have never shirked responsibility in my life and do not intend to start now," Lionel told her with a certain intensity in his voice, so that when he cut her off it did not quite occur to her to continue. Especially when she could see a matching blaze in his eyes. "This is a pointless conversation to have in the absence of any tests and the cool comfort such scientific fact inevitably provides, Geraldine. But I will ask you this. Who exactly is this cousin of yours that you believe I treated so shabbily?"

And then, because he actually looked as if he wanted to know, Geraldine found herself wishing that was a simpler question. Or one that even now, all these months later, long after Seanna had finally gone to her rest, she could actually answer with some authority.

She told herself she wasn't entirely sure she even *wanted* to open up Seanna's wounds to this man, when he'd already proved he could not be trusted to take care of them. Or her.

On the other hand, she had gone to all this trouble to find him. And was now married to the man, if he was to be believed. That she did not intend to honor any part of a ceremony she still couldn't quite believe had taken place did not make her any less married. Not if it was real. That was a curveball she hadn't seen coming.

She was beginning to deeply regret that she had charged into this whole situation so thoughtlessly. There had been no need to disrupt that wedding. She could have made an appointment with this man or one of his minions, as her mother had suggested repeatedly on the plane. But Geraldine had decided that the situation called for *a little bit* of drama. Surely the man deserved it after what he'd done.

I hope you're happy now, she told herself, in a voice that sounded uncannily like her mother's.

Because she really did know best, it seemed. Entirely too much of the time. No wonder she was Geraldine's favorite person.

Still, Geraldine had never been any sort of shrinking violet and it wasn't as if she could rewind and start the day anew. What was done was done and now all there was left to do was make the best of things.

She fully intended to do just that, no matter what it took.

Geraldine had promised Seanna she would, and *she* was a woman who kept her promises. So she squared her shoulders, adjusted her glasses once more for good luck and courage, and forced herself to meet his gaze as directly as ever.

Maybe more, because he clearly hadn't *seen* Seanna before. He'd seen only what she'd become, Geraldine assumed. Only what the life she'd chosen had done to her.

But she wanted him to know the person her cousin had been beneath all that. The person who should have lived long enough to raise her own baby.

The person who deserved far more than his callous abandonment.

"Seanna was a magical child," Geraldine told him fiercely, though she was mindful that men dismissed any hint of emotion should they hear it—so she forced herself to keep that fierceness at as even a keel as possible. "I was nine when she was born. And though my family has never been particularly close, it was as if she had been created for me alone. I treated her like a living, breathing doll at first. Then as a miniature version of me. We only became closer as she grew. She told me things she would never dare to tell her parents. She told me of all the dreams she had that didn't seem to fit. All the fantasies she had of a life that was bright and happy and far less cold than her parents' house, which, it has to be said, makes the whole of Minnesota seem like a sunny beach by comparison."

She expected a man of such intense self-importance to betray his impatience as she told this tale. To hurry her along, or snap at her, or bite her head off in some other way as she laid out Seanna's story in the way she'd been practicing for weeks now, but Lionel did none of those things. He remained where he was, in that same confusing position in the seat beside her. His long, hard body in its finery exhibited some level of indolence, surely, yet everything about the way he looked at her was taut. Intense.

As if he listened the way it was rumored he did everything else.

With every part of himself.

Geraldine had the stray thought that no one in her entire life had ever paid such close attention to her. Not ever.

And she was not entirely sure she knew what to *do* in the face of it. She had the unworthy urge to laugh. Or simply close her eyes and tip herself toward him, as if that might *do something*—

It was obvious that the jet lag was messing with her once again.

She forced herself to carry on anyway, hoping that this time, *fainting* wasn't on the table and if it was, that he would leave her to it in her perfectly comfortable seat. "Seanna was a remarkably pretty girl. And I don't mean that she was simply cute, as so many little girls are. Most if not all little girls, in my opinion. But Seanna was so pretty that strangers would stop her in the streets to marvel at her looks." Geraldine smiled slightly, remembering the commotion her cousin had caused wherever she went. At five. Seven. Nine. To her mother's enduring horror, as if the attention Seanna drew to her so effortlessly was something she was *doing*, deliberately, to spite her. "She was so pretty that my aunt would often see people taking pictures of her on the sly, and not in a creepy way, but as if she was a piece of art. By the time she was a teenager, it was quite clear that she wasn't simply *pretty* any longer. Most of us hit those years and devolve into trolls of one variety or another, but not my cousin. She was already pretty, and then she became astonishingly beautiful, seemingly overnight. And it was more than the simple sum of her features. She had…something else. A kind of magnetism. I don't know how else to explain it. There was something about her that made whoever looked at her want to keep looking."

It amazed Geraldine how much it hurt to talk about her cousin, even when she'd truly thought that she'd put so much of this to rest. Because she had tried and tried. She'd read every book on grief and mourning she could get her hands on. Then she'd tried out the advice in each and every one of them.

Even before Seanna had died, Geraldine had been trying to come to terms with what had happened to her shooting star of a cousin.

Sometimes she wondered if watching the price of all that prettiness had left more of a mark on her than she liked to think.

Because now, face-to-face with the man she'd considered the bogeyman for so long, she felt that same old hitch inside of her. That same urge to collapse into the tears that threatened yet again, when she'd thought she'd left the sobs behind her.

It was talking about those early days, she thought. It was remembering what it had been like when Seanna was still such an innocent and had shined so brightly that the whole world had always seemed to hold its breath around her.

She really had been magic.

But Geraldine refused to give this man the satisfaction of seeing her cry about the things he'd helped do to her cousin.

She *refused*.

"When she was fourteen, she caught the attention of a talent scout on the streets of Minneapolis," she said instead, forcing herself to keep telling this story. Because she already knew no one else would, and that could not stand. She would not let it stand. "My aunt and uncle had no interest in letting their daughter get sucked into that sort of world. They have a very particular, very rigid sort of morality and certainly no imagination to speak of. They didn't think their daughter needed pictures taken of her, much less by strange people in far-off cities. The talent scout who found Seanna on the street gave her a card and my aunt not only ripped into pieces, she threw it into the fire." She sighed a little. "So maybe she has more imagination than I'm giving her credit for."

Geraldine studied Lionel's face for a moment then, as the car bumped along. She wondered why it was that neither sunlight nor shadows seemed to affect him. He didn't change at all. Worse, neither state was more or less revealing.

It was as if he was as enduring as stone.

There was no reason that idea should have made her shudder a little bit, but it did.

"But Seanna quite liked the idea of modeling." Geraldine smiled. "Or, if I know my cousin, she liked the idea of the attention. Because she was used to it, you see. That was the sort of beautiful she was. She was *used to* turning heads. She was used to fusses being made over her, wherever she went and whatever she did. Some people would shy away from that kind of thing, because it isn't about who a person is, is it? It's about what other people imagine a person might be. But Seanna wanted more. So she went ahead and tracked down the scout on her own, flew to New York when her parents thought she was on a school trip to Chicago, and the next time she spoke to her parents about modeling she did it with a lucrative contract in hand."

Geraldine blew out a breath then. She hated this part. Because it felt too much like selling out her family to a man who didn't deserve to know a single thing about them. And more, to a man who could not possibly understand the sorts of trials regular people faced. But there was nothing for it. This was the story, and she was telling it.

Besides. She had long since decided that simply being blood related to people did not mean that she was required to pretend they weren't problematic when they were. "My aunt and uncle weren't on board with their daughter getting swept up in something as squalid and showy as *modeling*, but there was a lot of money on the table. And they lived very modestly after my uncle was laid off. You might not understand this, but the sort of money that men like you might scoff at could change everything for regular people. And it did."

Geraldine laced her fingers together in her lap. Across the back seat that they shared, Lionel remained still. But there was still that intensity in the way he looked at her. She should have found that a barrier. She should have felt self-conscious, surely, but instead the seriousness of his expression made it easier to carry on.

"There was no warm-up, no testing of the waters," Geraldine told him. "Seanna became an instant sensation. She flew all over the world. She appeared in the pages of every magazine you can think of and a great many more I had certainly never heard of before. There were catwalks by the dozens. By the time she was eighteen she had worked with top designers and legendary photographers in Paris, Milan, New York, and anywhere else you can imagine. She was a stalwart at the fashion shows. In terms of a modeling career, she was an enormous success by any measure—if already worried about getting old. But her personal life was a disaster."

The man beside her said nothing. He certainly didn't issue any accusations, and yet Geraldine still felt her own guilt crash over her in some kind of heavy wave. There was an undertow there that she knew might sweep her under if she let it—

But she hadn't let it in some time. Today was no time to backtrack.

"It was very obvious that she wasn't well," Geraldine managed to say quietly. "It wasn't only that her appearance deteriorated so alarmingly—in person, I mean. Never in photographs. It was more concerning that she just…wasn't herself. She stopped her weekly calls home. She even stopped her daily calls to *me*. If we wanted to keep up with her we had to track her in the tabloids, where it became very clear that she'd learned how to party and was spending most of her time doing so in the company of very rich, very famous men who never seemed to care much for her. I used to ask her about the men she was linked with and every time it seemed to hurt her a little more. So I stopped asking. I regret that."

Lionel caught her gaze and held it one beat, then another.

Until Geraldine almost felt the need to rub that sensation away, as if he had actually reached out and made her heart pump with his own hand. A ridiculous notion by any measure and one she should have found alarming.

But she…didn't.

She felt a bit more severe as she pushed on. "Then, finally, she came home. Quite obviously unwell. Her mother and father, I regret to say, disowned her entirely within a day because of the substances she had become dependent on. All while claiming a certain moral high ground they certainly had not dithered over while taking her money. I took care of her myself."

"As you had when she was young," Lionel said in a low voice.

And it was shocking, somehow, to hear his voice just then. Much less to hear him tie such a neat bow around feelings that were still so raw. Geraldine felt shaken.

"I nursed her as best I could through her pregnancy, but she was very ill." She looked down at her fingers clenched in her lap, and swallowed. Hard. "There were concerns for the baby. Seanna did not get better. To be honest, I don't think she wanted to get better. And in the end, despite the doctors' best efforts, her poor heart gave out while she was giving birth. Her daughter was mercifully unharmed, though she did have some more issues in the first few months of her life than a baby should." She blew out a breath. "I took care of her, too."

"And did your cousin appreciate your martyrdom while she lived?"

It was a soft, almost silken question, and Geraldine took offense to it immediately.

"I think you mean to be unkind," she said, staring him down while her cheeks warmed with the force of what she told herself was temper. Not the embarrassment of hearing him say that word that her aunt and uncle had used to bludgeon her with. And that even her mother had been known to suggest might apply, more than once. "But I did not martyr myself to my cousin. I loved her. I was able to take a leave of absence from my job to care for her, because I wanted to. Because she had no one else. And because she trusted me. Unlike the rest of our family, I did not judge her. I still don't."

Lionel still did not seem to move a single muscle. He reminded her of a statue—somehow capturing a great predator in a stillness that made the viewer think only of the coming attack. "And how is it you have remained so free of the judgment that so many others seem immersed in, I wonder?"

"Because I read widely," she shot back at him. "It is impossible to read as many books as I have and remain narrow-minded. It's the very purpose of reading, I would even say." And when he only gazed back at her, almost as if he pitied her in some way, she felt strongly that he was not understanding the situation at all. "I'm a research librarian. It is literally my job to gather information without emotion or agenda, collate it, and present it. All facts, no feelings."

"But in this case, it would seem that feelings were at the forefront. Not facts." He lifted a distractingly well-shaped shoulder in that way of his that she had already grown to dislike. "I am familiar with a number of beautiful women, some of them models. This I have never denied, nor would I. But that does not make me father to the child of a teenage junkie, Geraldine."

She felt something inside her then, different from

before. It was much colder. Much darker. And beneath it, something else too—the faintest hint of a kind of…disappointment?

But that made no sense. She had come here expecting this man to be the villain he was. To be far more appalling than he seemed, in fact. She had been absolutely certain that she could dress him down as he deserved. Shame him if necessary. She was very good at both, and more, was never afraid to charge heedlessly toward the right thing no matter what.

She would get Jules the justice both she and her mother deserved, no matter what. Geraldine was resolved.

Yet Lionel was not acting in accordance with the script in her head. How was it possible to be disappointed that he was…exactly who she'd expected him to be?

The words *teenage junkie* swam about in her head, oddly specific.

"So," she said softly. "You do know her."

"Not in the way you imagine," Lionel replied, and for the first time, sounded slightly less than entirely calm. "One of my investments involves a rather famous couture house in Milan. I met your cousin. I can assure you, I'm not in the habit of sleeping with children. Or addicts, for that matter. It was…abundantly clear that she was unwell."

"And yet, of all the names she could have dropped, it was only yours she ever spoke to me." Geraldine scowled at him. "Why would that be? Why, even when she knew that her life was slipping away, would you be the only person she mentioned? Make that make sense."

"I cannot," he said.

But she didn't believe him.

It was something about the way his gaze shifted. That intensity diluted itself as she watched.

Lionel turned his attention to the streets around them, and away from her.

She didn't believe him, and a hard little knot seemed to form inside her, tying itself tight around that hint of disappointment, making it lead to something else entirely.

"I suppose the science will prove it one way or the other, then," she said, perhaps too forcefully. Funny, but she no longer cared. "I'm assuming you will have no objection to taking the necessary tests. To prove that what you say is true. A man like you should have no trouble having an answer to illuminate us all by the end of the day."

But when Lionel looked back at her, his expression had changed once again.

There was nothing there but stone and steel, and something implacable that was far more unyielding than either.

She had the strangest urge to hold her breath.

"I have no objection to a paternity test, Geraldine," he told her quietly enough, but there was nothing soft in it. And nothing soft in him, either, as far she could see. "But before we do any of that, you and I will have to come to an agreement about this marriage."

"I didn't agree to this marriage in the first place. Why would you think that I would do anything at all but divorce you at the first opportunity?" Geraldine sniffed. "In case I haven't made this clear, I don't think highly of you. I doubt very much that will change. Whether you are proved to be Jules's father or not."

But something she would not call a smile moved over his hard face then. The kind of curve that only made it clear that he was far more dangerous and significantly less indolent than she might have imagined so far.

And if she was perfectly honest with herself, she'd imagined a lot.

"I do not require your affection, Geraldine," he told her, quietly. Very, very quietly—which was in no way the same thing as *soft*. "In fact, I would prefer there be nothing of the kind between us. What I need is a wife. If that wife comes with a child in tow, all the better. I am perfectly prepared to make your life, and the child's life, remarkably easy."

That intensity was back in his gaze then, and it seemed to pierce straight through her, so that she really was holding her breath.

"I don't think—" she began, feeling as if things wanted to start spinning once again.

But Lionel Asensio only let that curve in his mouth deepen. "Nothing comes without a price,

Geraldine. I have certain requirements." Again, that shrug that was not a shrug at all. "And I will insist that they are met before I subject myself to any test, much less contribute to the raising of any child, no matter whose she is."

CHAPTER FOUR

LIONEL COULD TELL at once that Geraldine had not expected him to bargain with her.

This suggested to him that her research into him had not been as comprehensive as she claimed. For whatever else he was, he was known far and wide for his cold-blooded negotiations and his nonchalance in moments where other men crumbled.

Lionel did not crumble. He doubted he was capable of such a thing, and this should have been no different. He certainly shouldn't have found himself reaching for an uncharacteristic explanation, simply because...her green eyes widened in dismay.

He did not offer one, of course. But he was shocked that he even possessed the urge.

Since when had he tolerated the intrusion of someone else's feelings into the way he handled his business or himself?

But, of course, he knew the answer to that. The only person whose feelings he considered in any sort of ongoing fashion was his *abuelita*, because she had earned that consideration by making herself the only steadying influence in the whole of his life.

He had buried his interest in other people's inner workings and outer emotional performances with his father. And he had never looked back.

Green eyes should not have registered with him one way or the other.

He waited as the car pulled into the small, private airfield where his jet stood ready for takeoff. His man came to the door and opened it wide once the car rolled to a stop. Lionel thought that Geraldine would refuse to get out, but she didn't. Instead, she turned toward the door, looking more confused than anything else, and let the man help her climb from the vehicle.

But that confusion seemed to have fled her entirely when Lionel exited from the other side of the car and rounded it to stand by her side once more.

"Why are we at an airport?" she asked him, in what was not the friendliest of tones.

Lionel did not think she was in any particular mood to discuss the differences between proper airports in private airfield, so all he did was beckon toward the sleek little jet that waited there for them.

"We will return to Spain," he told her. "Tomorrow is my *abuelita*'s eightieth birthday, and you are her present."

Geraldine's mouth dropped open and he found himself unaccountably transfixed by it. The memory of that kiss upon the altar seemed to flash through him, though he could not have said why. It had hardly been a kiss at all. It should not have registered. It had been a simple press of his mouth to hers and yet here he was, consumed with a hunger he was certain he had never felt before.

He would remember something like this, cluttering up his head and making him begin to wonder if he might start living his life according to the dictates of his sex, like his father had done to such an extent that it was rumored his mother had deliberately infected herself with that virus to escape the shame of having married such a base philanderer.

Lionel had never believed that it had been deliberate, because he'd known his mother all too well. If from a distance, as he had been all of twelve when she died and she had been nothing if not careless with herself as well as with everything else. His father had lived some ten years longer, but that had only given him more time and space to wreck everything he touched.

All of these things he had lived through, these histrionic lives and deaths, and he was standing here in an Italian afternoon, obsessing over a plain woman's mediocre kiss.

He told himself it was because of the novelty, nothing more. She was not like the sort of women he had dallied with in the past. He had *married* her, for the love of God. He had never kissed a *wife* before. And certainly not *his wife*.

Perhaps a second thought—or five—was only to be expected.

"I can't have heard you correctly," she said, when he was certain she had heard him with perfect clarity. "You cannot mean to suggest… Why on earth would your grandmother want *me* as a present?"

"I have already told you this." He commended himself for his patience. "What my grandmother wishes is for me to be married and en route to producing the grandchild of her dreams. This has now been accomplished. Tomorrow I shall present you to her and all you will need to do is follow the appropriate script when that happens. Nothing could be easier."

And somehow, when that chin of hers rose, he was not surprised that she wished to defy him in this. "I'm not an actor. I'm not much for *scripts*."

He should have wanted to crush her, here and now, so that he might know he could depend on her tomorrow. He wanted to bend her to his will, as he did everyone and everything, many times without even having to try.

But then, of course, he would. Eventually, he knew he would.

There was no other outcome that he would allow.

And perhaps it was nothing so simple as defiance with this woman, who imagined herself on some kind of crusade. "Geraldine. You are not seeing the full picture."

"I believe I'm the only one standing here who is

actually aware of the full picture. As I have just been at pains to share with you."

"You have no bargaining chips," he told her, softly enough. "This should be obvious to you. Look where we are."

He watched a small frown increase in the space between her eyes as she did as requested, which felt perhaps too much like a victory. "I told you, I have a hotel on the outskirts of town. I don't know why you brought me here."

"I brought you here because it doesn't matter what you tell me." And he was proud of how he sounded then. Very nearly *gentle*, a word that anyone who had ever attempted to negotiate with him would have laughed at. Bitterly. "I have told you how it will be, and I assure you, that *is* how it will be. What you have to decide is how you wish the inevitable to take place."

She turned that frown toward him, and intensified it. "Inevitable?"

He could see the challenge in the way she asked that. And more, the clear inference that she believed that she was the one holding the cards here. That she thought she had some power over him.

And he almost admired that. He really did. Lionel couldn't recall the last time that he had ever had any kind of encounter with someone who didn't know precisely how much power he wielded, and more importantly, the vast power differential between him and them.

Once again, the novelty of this woman caught him off guard.

"We are already married," he told her patiently. Or close enough. "I understand you do not wish this to be true, but that does not make it any less so. Another truth you may find unpalatable is that we will be landing in Spain later this afternoon. I would prefer it if you boarded the plane of your own volition, but that is not required."

Her green eyes widened. "Is that a threat?"

"It is reality, Geraldine. This is what I'm trying to express to you." It was getting more difficult to maintain that patient tone with her, but he tried. He really did try. He reminded himself that while this might have been an unorthodox contract negotiation, that was still what was happening here. These things did not all have to happen in tedious boardrooms. "You have few choices here, so I would use the ones that you do have wisely."

"That sounds a whole lot like a threat, no matter how you try to dress it up."

"I do not have to dress it up. I would not bother to try." He shook his head, as if he felt sorry for her. He might have—had he not elevated her far above what must be deeply humble beginnings indeed. And yet asked so little in return. "I need a wife to present to my grandmother. This presentation will occur tomorrow. If you do as I ask, I will be only too happy to take whatever tests you like. And no matter what their result, I will make certain that this child is provided for in perpetuity."

He did not see how she could refuse or why she would wish to.

Yet the look on her face was not one of joy and acquiescence. Not by a long shot. "And if I do not play this bizarre game for you, a small child suffers. Is that what you mean to say?"

"That is a matter that is entirely under your control," he reminded her softly. "If you do not do as I ask, I will have to do what I can to convince my grandmother that our marriage is the sort she has long imagined for me, but without your input. I will tell her you are indisposed. She will ask, at once, if that means you are pregnant. And I will have no choice but to tell her that you are. What that means for you is that you will need to become so. Immediately."

When he had discussed something similar with the Cartwright heiress, it had been a far more arid conversation. He had not considered for a moment that any such necessary pregnancies would occur outside of a doctor's office.

It was odd that this woman made him wonder if, perhaps, it might be better to try things the old-fashioned way.

"You do realize that everything you're saying makes you sound like a raving madman, don't you?" she was demanding.

And what was funny was that her saying that felt a bit like a relief.

"I cannot deny it," Lionel said, aware that he sounded something bordering on *cheerful*, whatever that was. "These are the lengths that I am willing to go to please my grandmother and I will tell you, I do not really care if you think it mad."

Geraldine folded her arms in front of her and the way she looked at him took on a flinty sort of cast. "You have had many relationships with women."

Lionel blinked at that unexpected shift in the conversation. He tried to recall the last time anyone had surprised him so much, or at all, and failed. "I would say I have had a reasonable amount of relationships for a man of my age."

"What I mean is, you're known for always actually having relationships. Not merely strutting about like a rock star teeming with groupies." She made that sound a bit too much like *lice* for his comfort. And she was still talking. "That said, they are always quiet, these relationships of yours. Perhaps you'll allow a photo to be snapped at this or that high-profile event, but you do not run around making headlines regularly."

He considered her for a moment. "Certainly not. I prefer my personal life to be private."

Because it was impossible to do the kinds of business deals he did if everyone at the bargaining table knew every last lurid detail of his assignations. Lionel had always wondered why that wasn't more obvious to his peers.

Assuming, that was, that he, Lionel Asensio himself, could be said to *have* any peers.

"There are many men in your position who litter the trail behind them with one-night stands," Geraldine proclaimed, apparently answering that question herself. "You not only don't do that, ever, but the women you have these relationships with never take to the press when you're done with them."

"Perhaps," Lionel suggested lazily, "they are the ones who finish with me and therefore see no reason to discuss it with anyone."

And he could not have said why it pleased him that she laughed at that. "I don't think so."

"Dare I ask why we are delving so deeply into my romantic history?" When she didn't respond at once, he lifted a brow. "Could it be that you wish to fully inhabit your role as my wife? What an unexpected left turn, indeed."

Her frown deepened, but was undercut entirely by the way that flush betrayed her, yet again.

Something else he liked far more than he should.

"What I am trying to understand is why, if you were so desperate for a wife, you didn't marry one of your girlfriends," Geraldine said, sensibly enough. "Perhaps no one told you, given the rarefied circles you inhabit, but that's actually the typical way of things."

"Is it indeed?" He leaned back against the car,

never shifting his gaze from her upturned face. "And you are conversant on this topic because of the numerous husbands you have married and then discarded, I take it?"

She ignored that, though he saw her stand a little straighter. "I'm sure that you could have called up any one of them, indicated you had the slightest interest in them again, and they would have come running. You could have had a perfectly easy wedding to a woman who would not require threats to do your bidding… But maybe I'm missing something. Maybe all of these relationships were terrible, fraught with insurmountable minefields."

That hit a little too close to home, Lionel could admit.

The truth was, he was not well-suited to relationships, something he always told the women he dated before they embarked on one. But no matter how many times he explained that he did not believe in love and would not succumb to it, the same tired refrain played itself out in the same way. Each and every one of the women became more and more emotional, which he could not abide. And every time he finished with them because of this, they had professed their love and accused him of all manner of sins, most of which boiled down to the very thing he told them at the start. That he was unfeeling, uncaring. Heartless.

They were correct, he would always remind them. He had told them so himself.

How could anything else be expected from him? His father's emotions had resulted in trashed hotels from Barcelona to Fiji and back again. It had been operatic, the way the man had made the whole of the world a stage upon which anything and everything could be a fainting couch for his affairs, his schemes, his over-the-topic shamelessness in all things.

Lionel had closed himself off from all such emotional traps before he reached the age of eighteen.

"I do not wish to have discussions about my marriage," he told Geraldine instead of any of those things, because he could not see that psychoanalyzing himself was at all useful here. "And I do not wish there to be any doubt about who is in control of it."

She blinked at that, then blinked again, as if he'd told some kind of joke. "It is my understanding that there are many women who would sign up for that today. Happily."

"Relationships are always tricky." And Lionel couldn't seem to help himself. His brow lifted of its own accord. "As, naturally, you are well aware, given your vast breadth and depth of experience. It is very easy to promise things at the beginning, only to feel quite differently about them as time goes on. The beauty of a business arrangement is that feelings become carefully thought-out clauses, and squabbles are settled in advance with the power of a signature."

"I think that is a fiction that businesspeople like to tell themselves," Geraldine countered. "But corporations, business deals, and even contracts—these are all the work of human hands. It's just *people* wandering around pretending that they can take the human out of it."

Lionel did not quite smile at this odd hen of a woman lecturing him on business affairs. "I prefer to think of it as managing expectations."

The Italian sun beat down, warm for a fall afternoon, and he could feel his phone buzzing repeatedly in his pocket. It was alerting him to all the various fires that were no doubt being set right and left across his empire, because there were always fires and he was the only one who ever seemed able to take those blazes and lower them to a more manageable simmer.

The truth was, he enjoyed it.

But still he stood here on this airfield, carrying on this pointless conversation with a green-eyed woman in the ugliest dress he'd ever seen, when he knew— as she must—that all he needed to do was to lift the faintest finger and his security detail would sweep her onto his plane despite any objections she might have. He could do it himself, for that matter. She already knew that he was perfectly capable of lifting her up and toting her about.

Yet, looking at her now, she seemed to be under the impression that she was the one in control of this interaction.

And Lionel had been fascinated by power and authority for the whole of his life. That was what happened with a father like his had been, so decidedly unequal to the task. If not actively engaged in squandering whatever measure of either he had ever had, because he could.

Because he knew no one could stop him. Not his wife. Not his son. Not even his otherwise formidable mother.

Lionel's father had reveled in the things he could not be told not to do.

Perhaps it was unsurprising that Lionel himself had felt, from a very young age, that he had to earn what power he had. That he had to work hard so that he spoke with true authority and could not simply throw money at the problems he made, like his father and grandfather had always done.

That was wealth. And it was not the same thing as real power, no matter how it might look from the outside. No matter how many people tried to pretend otherwise because it was all they had.

But he found himself fascinated all the same by this woman who did not appear to notice that she possessed no power here, even less authority, and had not even the faintest hint of wealth to make it worth ignoring her lack.

If he was not mistaken, Geraldine Gertrude Casey seemed to think that whatever power she possessed was…innate.

How extraordinary.

"The hour is growing late," he told her then, instead of continuing to discuss her thoughts on the humanity of the corporate world he doubted she had ever experienced. "We are rapidly approaching the point of no return. And I regret to inform you, *mi querida esposa*, that if you force me into a position where I must flex my muscles here… I will."

And Lionel was something a little more than simply fascinated by how wholly unimpressed she looked at that statement. Because he could feel it. Everywhere.

"Here's the situation as I see it," Geraldine told him in that forthright way of hers. "For whatever reason, likely that you're entirely too rich for your own good, you have a lot of strange ideas. That would be your business, but you've made it mine. Luckily, my aims are simple. I've already told you why I am here, what I want, and what I intend to make sure I get out of this. You should also know that I'm not a complete moron."

"I do not recall suggesting otherwise."

"Haven't you? Still, you should know that my mother is aware of exactly what I was doing and where I was headed today. If I don't make it back to our hotel room, she will sound the alarm. And loudly."

If she expected a reaction, she was to be disappointed. "A pity, then, that when that alarm sounds you will be in Spain."

It took him a moment to place the sort of look she gave him then. He realized he had never seen such an expression on anyone's face, save one. His grandmother's.

For this woman he had married today was looking at him as if her patience was sorely tried. *Her* patience. With *him*. "That you still feel compelled to threaten me to take part in this ruined wedding of yours speaks volumes," she said, and even shook her head. "It seems to me that a person who could not hold on to his first bride might treat the second a bit more carefully. Imagine the conversation we could be having right now if you had laid out your objectives, allowed me to do the same, and we'd found a way to meet in the middle."

Her temerity was unmatched.

"This from the woman who was under the impression that I preyed upon an unwell teenager, then cast her aside when I was done with her." Lionel tried his best to keep his temper locked away, where it belonged. "Where, precisely, do you imagine the middle to be between that position and mine?"

"Does your grandmother have her hands on the purse strings? Is that why you feel the need to go to such theatrical lengths for her?"

"My grandmother is none of your concern."

Geraldine laughed. It sounded faintly triumphant. "Then I can't imagine why you'd want me to play this elaborate game of pretend to deceive her."

That was the moment that Lionel realized a great many things.

First, and most surprising, was that they had somehow...gotten close. He wanted to think it was her doing, but he was quite certain that she was in the exact same position, standing there with her arms crossed over the front of that floral monstrosity, glaring up at him. That meant that he must have been the one to move closer, so that he stood there above her, looking down, entirely too close—

As if, at any moment, he might reach out his hands and wrap them around her upper arms, and then—

And then...what? he asked himself.

That was when the second thing occurred to him. Namely, that they were standing out here in public. He had only seen his own men here, but that didn't mean there couldn't be others nearby. Because while it was true that he did not spend a lot of his time in the headlines, there were always paparazzi lurking about, hoping to sneak in a shot that might change things.

He could not recall a single time in his entire life that he had ever lost sight of that.

That he had ever forgot, for even one moment, who he was and what he represented to those who might use him for their own ends. Or even just his name.

Next thing you know, you will be cavorting about on appalling yachts in the Mediterranean, awash in C-list actresses and models past their prime, he told himself scathingly. *Is that what you want? To become the parody of your useless grandfather that your father was? To remind the entire world how and why the Asensio name became associated with everything tawdry for far too long before you?*

Lionel wanted no such thing. Not when his entire life had been an attempt to emulate the kind of quiet command of the family name and assets that his grandmother had always embodied so well.

He had no intention of letting that change now. No matter the strange pull this woman seemed to exert on him.

He signaled his men, then looked back at Geraldine. "If you are planning to make a choice that does not involve me throwing you over my shoulder and carrying you on board the plane myself, now is the moment."

"I will pass on Neanderthal displays, thank you," Geraldine said. Stiffly, he thought. She sniffed, then unfolded her arms at last—but only so she could shove her glasses back up her nose.

A gesture he told himself he found deeply irritating. That was surely the reason he couldn't seem to look away while she did it.

"Wonderful," he said smoothly, as if he had heard nothing insulting at all. "As I mentioned earlier, there are certain scripts that we will need to follow—"

"Listen to me," Geraldine said then, cutting him off. Another moment so outside his experience that he could only stare back at her, too astonished to otherwise react. "Jules is what matters to me. Not your grandmother. Not even really you, though I think you should have to pay for what you did. There is the issue of responsibility, but there's also another issue, of restitution. That's why I'm here. And the only reason I'm even considering playing ridiculous games with you is because that sounds a great deal like the fastest way to get Jules what she deserves. Do you understand me?"

Lionel gazed down at her for what felt to him like a long, long while. "Do I seem to you to be…deficient in understanding?"

She only glared. Again. He had never known a woman to glare much at all in his presence, unless she was related to him. Even then it had never been so often.

"I will need you to say it, please," she told him.

As if she did not find what he had said already sufficient because she found him untrustworthy in some way. As if she, a nobody from nowhere—and that was being generous—needed more. From him.

From *him*.

And that was the moment, Lionel realized. The moment that everything shifted, little as he might have wished it to.

He knew too many things then that he wished he did not.

Too many things he would have taken back, if he could.

"I understand completely, Geraldine," he said, from between his teeth.

And he watched as she inclined her head, like royalty, and then actually beckoned for him to precede her to his own damn plane so she could trail along after him, as if this entire situation was hers to command.

She was wrong about that, of course.

But it was that moment that Lionel kept returning to. As the plane took off, and Geraldine stopped scowling at him only long enough to fall asleep before the plane completed its climb into the sky.

It was that moment he thought about over and over as he studied the circles beneath her eyes that suggested she really was tired, and not simply narcoleptic. Or simply trying out a new form of defiance as best she could.

He kept studying her, noting that in sleep her glasses slid down even farther, so that they nearly reached the tip of her nose and then, when she shifted in her seat, fell to her chin. Where they hung from her ears and should have made her look ridiculous. Perhaps she did. But Lionel found himself cataloging, instead, what appeared to be mounting evidence that he had somehow stumbled upon a diamond in the rough.

He already knew that she was not as shapeless as she seemed to wish she was. He had discovered that firsthand. But now he could see that she had the potential to be quite beautiful, in her own way. Now that she was not glaring and scowling, rolling her eyes, or making those disapproving faces of hers.

She did not look as if she had ever cared very much for her hair, save that shampoo she used that smelled like beachside holidays. But it was a more interesting shade of brown than some and if he wasn't mistaken, had a bit of a natural wave to it as well. There were stylists who could do wonders with such a canvas. Especially when her skin was smooth and her nose was straight. Her lips, as he had discovered, were firm and not overly thin. Her teeth had looked straight enough. She might even have a nice smile, not that he would know, as she had not aimed one in his direction.

Lionel could work with this. He could make her over into a woman resembling the sort his grandmother would expect him to have married—because convincing her was what mattered. There was no way that his sharp-eyed *abuelita* would believe, for even one moment, that he had accidentally become besotted with a woman who wore sofas as dresses and went about *scowling* at people through dark-framed glasses that made her face look misshapen.

Geraldine possessed the one thing he knew his grandmother wanted for him above all else. Lionel was so certain that he would bet the Asensio name and the whole of his fortune on the fact that she was completely innocent. His grandmother would approve of that, he knew.

But she would not believe for one moment that it was a real marriage—the kind she had lectured him extensively that she wanted for him—if he brought Geraldine to her looking like this.

My marriage to your grandfather was arranged, she had told him on her last three birthdays. *As was your mother's to your father. I would call neither a success. You must do better,* mi nieto. *I want something real for you.*

What you want, Abuelita, is less scandal attached to the family name, Lionel had replied each time.

The older woman had eyed him, amused. *I am not opposed to your happiness, child. I simply cannot trust you to find it yourself.*

Lionel shot off the necessary messages to his assistants, so they might have the appropriate people in place when the plane landed in the Asensio estate in the hills of Andalusia. Tucked between the olive orchards and the vineyards, gorges in one direction and white hilltop villages in the other, the estate had stood for far longer than the reputation of two late and largely unlamented men who had done their best to dismantle what their ancestors had built.

The selfishness. The waste. The complete inability to think of anything beyond self-gratification, no matter the cost—

But he ordered himself to shut that off. It was the past.

And he would not do the same as they had done. He would use this strange woman he had married as the weapon she needed to be to achieve his aims.

It started with the transformation he wished Geraldine to undergo before tomorrow, so that his grandmother could live out the rest of her life in ease and comfort—insofar as she allowed herself such weaknesses—and pay far less attention to her only grandson's personal affairs.

But when that was done, he returned again to that same moment, there beside a car in Italy.

Because that was when he'd known.

That despite his best intentions—and whether she took to her transformation or did not—this marriage was not going to be any kind of business arrangement, after all.

Because Lionel intended to have Geraldine beneath him, in every way a man could, and soon.

CHAPTER FIVE

IF GERALDINE HAD known what Lionel had planned, she thought crossly some hours later, she would have flatly refused to help him.

She'd woken up as the plane started its descent into Spain. She stared out at white buildings clinging to hillsides that gleamed in the September sun. As the plane got lower and lower, there were rolling fields, vineyards and olive orchards, and then a grand sort of Spanish-style house that took over the better part of a valley hidden away between two rolling, unspoiled hills.

It was so beautiful that it actually made her chest hurt.

If she was more fanciful, she might have allowed herself to brood on the notion that it felt like coming home—but she wasn't. So she didn't.

"I have to let my mother know where I am," Geraldine informed Lionel once the plane's wheels hit the ground. When really, she just wanted to know if the baby was okay. It wasn't that she didn't think her mother could care for Jules, because of course she did. It was just that she liked doing the caring herself. "Otherwise, as I said—"

"Yes, yes. Alarms will sound, and so on." He did that thing with his hand that was somehow an invitation even while it was dismissive. Maybe aristocratic sorts learned such things while ordering the nursery staff about from their cradles. "By all means, call whoever you like."

And then made it clear that he had no intention of giving her any privacy to do so.

"What you mean you've gone off to *Spain*?" Her mother had sounded astonished by that news when she picked up the call. And fair enough. Geraldine could hear Jules babbling to herself in the background, sounding sunny and happy, and had to close her eyes against the piercing sort of longing that washed over her. Especially because her mother was still talking. "I thought we came here for a very specific purpose. Not a sudden Grand Tour when we've barely landed."

"Wonderful," Geraldine had said brightly. "I let you know when I'll be back just as soon as I can."

And then she'd finished the call, feeling guilty that she'd abandoned both her mother *and* the baby.

"I prefer business arrangements," Lionel had said in that dark, stirring manner of his, as if he was not only aware of all the little fires that kicked up inside of her at the sound of his voice, but intended to light them with his own hands. As if he knew every last contour of the things she felt, when as far as she could tell, he was made of ice. "As I said."

She made herself smile. "Once again, you seem to be missing the part where this is something humans do. Having relationships are what life is supposed to be about."

"Alternatively, you could arrange your life to serve you," Lionel had replied. "This is what I choose to do."

And then he had shown her what he meant.

She had walked down the folding stairs that served as the plane's Jetway to find herself on yet another private airfield, this one even more remote than the one they'd stood on back in Italy. And she may or may not have dreamed about being that close to him, hardly aware of the words that were coming out of her mouth because she was too busy gazing up at him, wondering what it would feel like to surge up a little higher and press her mouth to his—

But she had very little time to reflect on the difference between Italian and Spanish private airfields, because she was swept up into a noisy crowd almost immediately.

They all spoke too quickly, and not to her. They were all dressed in black, and despite Geraldine's talk about human behavior, they appeared to be treating her as if she was something like cattle.

Her hair was let down by someone, while another held strands between his fingers, letting out a stream of remarks that she did not have to speak Spanish to know were not exactly admiring. Worse, another man staggered back and clasped a hand to his chest in what appeared to be not entirely feigned shock at the sight of her dress. So dramatically that he had to be propped up by the woman beside him, who spoke rapidly to him, as if attempting to convince him to continue breathing long enough to fix the situation.

It did not take long to understand that there was indeed a situation, and the situation was her.

"If I wanted a makeover," Geraldine snapped over the din, finding Lionel's slightly too amused gaze as he climbed into a separate, clearly far quieter car beside hers, "I would give myself one."

"No need," he told her smoothly. "We will meet for dinner, after my people determine whether or not miracles can be performed. And then we will go from there, you and I."

She had felt rather more let down than she should have when he'd actually got into his vehicle and drove off into the spectacular countryside that surrounded them.

Geraldine was forced to acknowledge that she was a little more focused on Lionel Asensio than she should have been. When she knew full well what kind of man he really was. And worse, what he was capable of doing. Or not doing.

"Do any of you speak English?" she asked once she'd been packed into her own car, where the horde descended upon her once again.

"Of course we all speak English," said the woman

nearest her, not bothering to look up as she inspected Geraldine's nails. "But until we have something nice to say, we will speak Spanish."

And she was as good as her word.

Geraldine found herself carted off to some kind of small cottage. Though it could only be called such a thing—small or cottage—when considered next to that sprawling house she had seen on the flight in. It had more rooms than her tidy little two-bedroom house that she'd been so pleased to buy a few years ago, so she could feel like an adult at last.

It had taken Jules to make her realize that there was so much more to feeling like an adult than the little house, if that was what she wanted. Geraldine had always thought that she didn't want those things. That a life of books and friends, quiet joys, and the pleasure of her own company were enough. They had been enough.

Certainly the fast, loud, high life that Seanna had led had never appealed.

But then Geraldine had taken Jules into her arms at the very moment of her birth, and had held on to her tight ever since.

Her aunt and uncle had refused to get involved in what they called Seanna's catastrophically bad choices. Even after Seanna died, they could not be swayed to take the slightest notice of their grand-child. They'd advocated for Seanna's child to be given up for adoption, so that no one in the family would be forced to remember any of the unpleasantness unless they wanted to. Geraldine and her mother had tried as best they could to make them see reason, but they could not be swayed. And in the end, Geraldine had prevailed.

Because she had held that wriggling little creature against her neck. She had breathed in her first cries. And she'd understood, in a terrible and wonderful wave, that she would do anything and everything—always—to keep that little girl safe.

She could admit to herself that it was also possible that taking care of Jules allowed her to do it all over. To do it better this time, as she wasn't a nine-year-old. And sometimes, late at night, she would stare at her ceiling after putting the baby down and wonder if one of the things that made caring for Jules such a no-brainer for her was that it allowed her to feel a great deal like the savior she hadn't been able to play for her cousin.

Or even the big sister she'd always wanted to be, though her parents had tried. They hadn't been able to have any other children, so when Seanna had come along, Geraldine had adopted her as her very own.

And the truth was, she knew only too well that people couldn't save each other. They could only save themselves, and help those who asked for it. *If* they asked for it.

But she felt nothing like a savior today. If anything, Geraldine felt like a child herself. Or a mannequin. The scrum of stylists took her over. She was marched into a bathroom suite and her hair was washed. She was given a manicure and a pedicure at the same time that one of the stylists fussed over her hair with scissors, a comb, and the light of battle in his gaze.

In the next room, she could hear the rest of them discussing her, but she wasn't allowed to even look at herself when her hair was done. Too busy were they marching her behind a screen, demanding that she remove her dress to put on a flimsy little robe before hauling her back out from behind the screen and making her stand on the little platform.

Once again, a tide of rapid Spanish threatened to sweep her away.

"It is not so bad," said the original woman who had spoken to her in the car, smiling slightly. "Everyone is pleased that it is only the dress that made you look so terrible."

"I like that dress," Geraldine protested. "It's comfortable."

"*Comfortable* is another word for surrender," the man who had nearly fainted on the airfield chimed in then, also in English. "And if one must surrender, better to do it so stylishly, so elegantly, that in retrospect your surrender might look a little bit like a victory, after all."

And then no one spoke to her again as they worked.

There were no mirrors in the room, a kind of graceful salon. Up on her little raised dais, Geraldine had a view out the windows. It was beautiful. The rolling hills, the incoming autumn season, the bright sky.

She had no idea why it made her want to cry. That was how peaceful it was.

They made her put on one thing, then another, and then debated among themselves as they made her turn this way, then that. There was a seamstress on hand who took whatever garments gained the approval of the crowd and tailored them on the spot, so that, in the end, everything that she was approved to wear fit her to exquisite perfection.

A notion that made her...uneasy.

"Do I get to look at your masterpiece?" she asked when a great many hours had passed, the sun was setting over the hills outside, and they had finally decided that they could take her to Lionel.

"There is no particular need," replied the man who led her through the cottage that was no cottage at all, with its rooms upon rooms, halls filled with whitewashed walls and art, and the hint of bookshelves heaving beneath the strain of too many volumes she itched to get her hands on. The man beside her sniffed. "You must know that your opinion has not been solicited, Señora Asensio."

But even as he called her that name that she could not accept was hers, he slowed as they walked into a sort of atrium and nodded his head toward the decorative mirror that took over the better part of one wall.

Where Geraldine saw, to her horror, that they had made her beautiful.

Inarguably so.

"Oh, no," she whispered. "This is a disaster."

"What did I tell you?" cried the man beside her. He clucked at her as if she had disappointed him, personally. "*Callate*, if you please. We are artists, you are our creation, and this has nothing to do with what *you* think. You would wear that dress before *la ilustrísima* señora Doña Eugenia Lourdes Rosario herself, and this we cannot have."

And then he ushered her with a rather ungentle hand on the small of her back, through the glassed-in atrium with orchids blooming madly and then outside, where Geraldine stopped dead.

Because there was a bit of a secret garden here, back behind this place. A walled-in, overgrown, glorious patch of paradise, where flowers bloomed everywhere she looked, the sweet air was scented with mysterious things she could not quite identify, and there were a thousand candles fighting off the dark.

And in the center of it all stood Lionel.

Looking at her with a certain *intent* that made the world seem to spin again.

Oh, no, Geraldine thought again.

And not because she worried that she might faint. More that she was afraid that…she wouldn't.

"I hope you're satisfied," she said, her voice sharper than planned.

She was too aware of…too much. The sultry Spanish night, flowing around her like the kind of caress she did not wish to think about in this man's presence. The scent of so many flowers, dancing on the evening breeze. The last of the sunset itself, a pageant of deep pinks, burnt oranges, and deep indigos that she would have watched like its own movie under any other circumstances.

But there was no looking away from Lionel.

Just as there was no pretending that there was some other reason for the sudden breathlessness she felt while she did.

"*Satisfied* is not the word I would choose," he said, the low heat of his voice a counterpoint to that dark blaze in his eyes. They looked less like the color of dark coffee in the evening light, with so many candles flickering everywhere, and more like something significantly less prosaic. Very old whiskey, for example. Smoky and dangerous.

Geraldine remembered, then, that she had stopped dead in her tracks.

It was harder than it should have been to force herself to walk toward him, when it felt so much like walking to the edge of a very steep cliff and hoping against hope that she could balance there.

She became suddenly and shockingly aware of the clothes she was wearing. It was as if she hadn't been present in that room as all those people had swirled around her, dressing and undressing her as if she really was nothing more than a canvas. She'd sighed when they'd let this particular dress float over her shoulders, then had sewn her into it. And it had been the particular fit of the garment that caught her eye first when she'd actually seen her reflection.

That had been bad enough.

But this was worse. Much worse.

Because she understood with every step that Lionel's reaction was catastrophic.

He was not looking at her the way he had before, as if she was a very faintly amusing novelty that he could use to his own ends. He was not looking at her in that pitying way, the way she was sure he had been when she'd found herself in his arms. He was not looking at her with that scowl that had demanded, before he'd said a word, that she think better of her own temerity in laughing at his misfortune.

The look on his face now was something else altogether.

And she hated that it had nothing to do with her, and everything to do with her appearance. An appearance that had required an entire team to create.

"I do not understand." And there was a hoarse note in Lionel's voice as she came to stand before him, there where a small table had been set, with crystal glassware reflecting the candlelight. "That hideous garment you wore today makes no sense. I do not understand what would make you do such a thing. When you could look like this."

Geraldine glared at him. "Because that hideous garment is comfortable." She waved a hand down the length of her body, too aware of the way his gaze tracked the movement. "Does it look to you as if this is comfortable?"

The dress was a column of vibrant color that clung

to her figure. And Geraldine had no illusions about herself or her charms. She had grown up with Seanna. She knew only too well that her own form was not fashionable in the least. Her proportions were much too generous. She had accepted that long ago. Happily enough.

But she was fully aware that on any occasion she mistakenly wore something that presented her figure so all could see, there were…reactions.

Too many reactions.

And she knew what followed on from such reactions. Her cousin's entire life was a cautionary tale.

Besides, Geraldine had never wanted to shine like that. She'd wanted to be smart and capable, thank you, and back in the horror of adolescence it had seemed very clear to her that she had to choose. One or the other.

So she had.

It didn't help that tonight they had done whatever they'd done to her hair, so that it seemed glossier and softer. It swirled around her shoulders, making her look as sultry as the Spanish night all around them, when she would far prefer to forget about it and twist it up and out of her way. It was irritating when it heated against the back of her neck.

Nor did it help that they had taken care of all the little details she found too annoying to ever do herself. The manicure that made her hands look somehow less capable than before. The pedicure that had made her feet feel overly soft and fragile. The high-heeled sandals with delicate straps that were suitable for walking extremely short distances, if that.

There was nothing practical about a single thing she was wearing. Including the necklace they'd clasped around her neck with a single diamond solitaire set to sparkle just there, above the place where the dress ended, so that it was impossible not to look at the thrust of her breasts and the hollow between them. Not to mention her entirely bare shoulders, which someone had dusted with a powder that had made her gleam in that hallway, and likely made her outright sparkle here in the candlelight.

She knew, too, that they had taken shocking liberties with her face. Left to her own devices, Geraldine did not wear color on her lips. It only called attention to them, making them seem plumper and glossier than they ought to have been. She had never been one to take such care with her eyes, elongating her lashes, rubbing on creams and shadows, and adding layers of mystery and shadow so that her green eyes were far more inviting than necessary. When they were already *green*, for God's sake.

There's no way around it. This was a disaster.

If he was looking at her like this, if this was all he saw, how could she force him to face what he'd done? That required fortitude, not fashion. She was sure of it.

"Comfortable," Lionel was saying, echoing the word she'd used as if he had never heard it before. He said it again, managing to sound even more baf-

fled. "Surely you realize that comfort is for those who could not achieve what you have naturally, yes? It is a trap at best."

"It is a necessity if a person lives through winters in Minnesota," Geraldine retorted. "I can assure you that I have very little call to go prancing around dressed like this when the weather is below zero, my car won't start unless it's hooked to a heating block, and layers upon layers of cold-weather gear are required to step outside."

"Those are no longer your concerns," he told her, in the silken sort of way that made all the hairs all over her body seem to stand on end in warning. It was a *warning*, she told herself. "For you are now the wife of an Asensio, and there will be no more scrabbling about in cold winters, concerning yourself with such menial tasks."

"If that's the sales pitch you think you should be leading with, I have some news for you," Geraldine replied with admirable calm, she thought, given the state of her pulse. "You've read this situation wrong. Why would I have the slightest interest in the kind of superficial glamour that killed my cousin? Or the man who helped engineer it?"

She had sense that something in him hardened, but all he did was study her for a moment, then step back and indicate that she should take her seat at the table.

Geraldine felt like a trap was closing around her. As if she'd stuck her arm into a terrifying set of steel jaws and the only way out might be to gnaw the whole thing off—

Then again, she thought, repressively, *it could be that you're simply hungry, since the last thing you ate was a selection of stale nuts on that plane.*

"Perhaps it would be better if we hold off on accusations and character assassinations, *mi querida esposa,*" Lionel said as she pulled herself together and took her seat. As he stood there and helped her into it when she needed no such aid, then held the back of the chair to slide it into the table, so that she felt him all around her. As if he was touching her when he was not. "After all, I would not wish you to feel embarrassed when the results prove my innocence."

He looked entirely too sure of himself for her peace of mind when he rounded the small table and took the seat opposite hers.

"Even if the results do come back and prove that you're Jules's father, I won't feel embarrassed," she declared then, though she wasn't really sure that was true. But what mattered was that she *sounded* sure, she told herself. "I told you the reasons why I sought you out. They remain valid. If you are named incorrectly, that only means that I will have some follow-up questions for you."

"Geraldine," he said, a different note in his voice—or maybe it was just the way he said her name, making it a lilting thing. A scrap of a song, much the way his own name sounded in his language, three lovely syllables instead of something that rhymed with *vinyl*. "This all sounds like a great many words and attempted diversions to cover the fact that you are quite beautiful. And that you have clearly gone to great lengths to hide it."

It was only now, sitting at the table, that she realized what she should have noticed immediately. They had taken her glasses away at some point while washing her hair and had never given them back. The realization was a relief, she found. *No wonder* she found everything so sultry, so atmospheric.

Not that it helped her now. She couldn't see details well in the distance, but now that she was sitting with only this table between her and Lionel, she could, regrettably, see that he looked even better up close.

Not better, she lectured herself. *More dangerous. Everything about him is a calculated seduction, and you know where it ends.*

But she was dismayed to find that knowing such things did not set her straight as much as it should have. Because her body did not appear to be getting the message that she was not to find him attractive.

"I'm not beautiful," she told him matter-of-factly. "My cousin was beautiful."

"It is not all one thing or the other." Lionel leaned back in his chair and the way he looked at her seemed to happen from the inside out, making everything within her *hum*. "Is this what you meant when you spoke about shying away from beauty because it is only on the surface? Because it is not who you are?"

Geraldine barely remembered saying that, though

it sounded very much like something she *would* say. She didn't understand that tightening in her chest then, as if the very idea that this man had actually paid that much attention to her while she was speaking made her…some kind of stranger to herself, as if the woman she could see reflected in his gaze was more *her* than she had ever been.

She did not care for that at all.

Or maybe she was worried that she did.

"True beauty is not something that can be hidden away with a pair of glasses and an unflattering dress," she said quietly. "That's a Hollywood movie. The reality is that I have a certain shape, that's all. I find that I very rarely like the attention that shape brings me. But then, unlike fancy billionaires and famous models, I do not find that I enjoy very much attention at all."

He seemed to look at her for a long while, and that humming inside her was turning into something more like a seismic episode, but still he kept on. And she wanted to break this moment apart before it broke her, but she couldn't seem to open her mouth. She couldn't seem to do anything at all but look back at him, the harsh beauty he wore so easily seeming even more magnetic, even more tempting, in the soft touch of the candlelight.

"Very well," he said at last, as if something had been decided.

He did something with one hand, and suddenly their private little garden was filled with two staff members who managed to make it seem as if there were at least triple of them. They bustled about and when they left, there was wine in the glasses, candles between them, and platters of food that smelled so good she had a moment where she thought she might actually weep.

"The food is a selection of local delicacies. Andalusia is known for its food, and my cook is the best," he told her, and not in a way that suggested he was exaggerating to compliment his chef. But in a way that suggested that it was a quantifiable fact. He inclined his head. "Eat, Geraldine."

And for a while, that was exactly what she did. The flavors were seductive. The dishes played with savory and sweet in different combinations, like a complicated dance. She only wished that her appetite was big enough to eat every last morsel on the table.

But Geraldine did not realize until some time had passed that she'd miscalculated. Because there was something too intimate about sitting in the candlelight, as the sky darkened above them and then gave itself over to the night. There was something about the way the candles danced in the little bit of breeze, the only music the soft touch of it as it went. And how the act of eating together, in silence, made whatever this was between them feel fraught. Deeper than it was. Almost as if—

But she could not allow herself to think these things. Not with this man who might very well be responsible for what had happened to her cousin. Not when Jules was her first and foremost responsibility these days—as she should be. The baby was the point of all of this, not whatever she felt on a night breeze in the company of this man.

She put down her fork when it occurred to her that she had started to think about it as if it might not be true. As if it might not be him.

As if she was tempted to believe him.

Lionel was lounging in the chair across from her, toying idly with a wineglass on the table before him, though his gaze remained trained on her.

"You seemed to have enjoyed the cuisine of my country," he said, after some while had passed. An eternity or two, to her mind, caught up like that in his dark, gleaming gaze. "I am glad."

And Geraldine had never felt like this before. As if there was something effervescent stuck in the pit of her stomach, like a kind of indigestion—only she knew that it was not the type that would make her sick. On the contrary, it felt a great deal more like joy.

She suddenly found that she had a great deal more sympathy toward her cousin's choices than she ever had before. She hadn't judged Seanna, that was true. But she hadn't understood her, either.

Suddenly, what had not made any sense to her before seemed clear.

And she wanted to lash out at him, because she felt precarious, as if despite the fact that she was sitting down with a table between her and him, she was still standing on that cliff she'd imagined before. Arms wheeling, legs shaking.

She didn't like it.

But she also couldn't quite bring herself to let the sharp edge of her tongue fly. "Every bite was exquisite," she said. Truthfully.

And that wasn't a compliment, she assured herself. It was the simple truth. And the fact that the simple act of eating with him seemed far too sensual, well. Perhaps that was something she needed to work on. Within herself.

"I am delighted to hear it," Lionel murmured.

And when he lifted his gaze just slightly, she found herself sitting up straighter, which in no way shifted that fizzy thing deep inside her. If anything, it made it grow. It was something about the way the candlelight caressed the harshly perfect lines of his face. It was the way he looked at her, pitiless and sure.

It made her want to giggle. Then melt.

"Now," Lionel said. "It is time you and I discuss exactly will happen tomorrow, exactly what you will do, and what penalties you might expect if you do not obey me."

Geraldine had never wanted to obey anyone. She had never considered herself *obedient* in any way.

But the way Lionel looked at her now, she was reconsidering her stance.

She had to shake herself slightly to make that wondrous aching and sparkling thing that was taking her over loosen its grip. Though she wasn't sure it worked.

"Tomorrow is my grandmother's birthday," Lionel was saying. "She was never shy or retiring in any way, but the advance of her years has made her even less discreet than she was. You must be prepared for this. She will ask you whatever she likes. She delights in being provocative. I expect that you will handle whatever she throws at you with humor and grace."

"This might come as a surprise to you," Geraldine replied, though it was harder to sound dry and amused than she would have liked, "but I have actually interacted with eighty-year-old women before."

"I doubt very much that the sweet pensioners you might have stumbled over in your library have anything in common with a woman some have called the unofficial queen of Spain," Lionel replied with a hint of amusement in his voice that made Geraldine feel something a little too much like foolish. "You may have a distaste for wealth, but you must not show it. In your American way, imagine yourself somehow equal to an aristocrat, but that is not a position my grandmother shares. Doña Eugenia Lourdes Rosario Asensio can trace herself and her bloodline back across untold centuries, and that means something to her. You will do well to remember that."

"So far she sounds like a gorgon." Geraldine only shrugged when that brow of his rose, signaling his disapproval. "Once again, I am forced to wonder why it is you are so determined to do her bidding."

"She is the only woman on earth whose bidding I will ever do," Lionel returned, and there was something about the way he said that. It was like some kind of premonition, or foreboding.

Geraldine told herself she was being absurd. "Then what I would like is practical, concrete advice on how I'm expected to behave tomorrow if I'd like you to take responsibility for the child you might have created." She told herself that she liked the way his eyes darkened at that. And that her growing certainty that she was being set up to disappoint him was a good thing, no foreboding premonitions necessary.

That's what you need, she lectured herself. *To be nothing he wants. To embarrass him. So you remember what's actually happening here. Not whatever it is you think you* feel *tonight.*

And so she only half listened as Lionel began to outline the sort of customs and expectations, manners and protocol that a woman like his grandmother would expect. The party was not going to be some intimate gathering, or visit in a care home, as she might have been imagining. *La ilustrísima* señora Doña Eugenia Lourdes Rosario liked to celebrate herself in style.

"You do not appear to be as overwhelmed by these things as I would expect," Lionel pointed out after he had talked for some while, and he did not sound pleased by that. "As would be perfectly appropriate for a person in your situation."

"I'm not worried," Geraldine replied, and tried a

wave of her own hand to indiscernible effect. "I can assure you that I'm perfectly capable of picking up the correct fork a dinner party and managing myself decently enough that I do not embarrass anyone in my vicinity."

"Because of your vast experience at grand affairs of this nature?"

"Because, once again, I have read across a wide array of topics," Geraldine said lightly. Or perhaps not quite so lightly, because even she could hear the edge in her voice. "I have likely read a great many more books about customs and propriety than you."

"I admire your confidence," he replied in a way that made it clear that he did not.

And Geraldine couldn't seem to get a handle on all the sensations competing for her attention, deep inside, so she decided it was time she stopped trying. She pushed back from the table, standing up and smiling a little bit as she looked at him, as if she was the one in charge of this. "I will expect that by the end of this dinner party of yours, a fleet of doctors, scientists, whatever you like, will descend upon you and Jules. And that they will answer the question of whether or not you're her biological father once and for all. That's the only thing I'm interested in. If I have to make sparkling conversation with snooty aristocrats to make that happen, that seems a small price to pay indeed."

She was not prepared for the way Lionel rose, then. She'd miscalculated once again, she realized too late, because once he did they were suddenly standing entirely too close to each other.

Much too close, something in her seemed to cry out, its own alarm.

In a secret garden filled with candlelight and the scent of night-blooming flowers on the breeze.

"I assume I'm to stay here," she said, dismayed that her voice seemed to get higher and higher with every syllable. She cleared her throat. "I'm sure someone mentioned that this was the guest cottage. I assume you stay, awash in your magnificence, somewhere significantly more spectacular."

Lionel studied her in the candlelight, and it made everything inside her feel…fragile.

Except it was far too raw for that.

And somehow she knew exactly what he was going to say. Before he uttered a word.

"This is my home, Geraldine." She heard the words he said, but the way he looked at her made them *feel* like something else. "I am devastated that you do not find it up to your standards."

"I'm sure it will be fine." And she sounded more frigid than she might have wished, because her head was spinning. She didn't want to stay in the same place as this man. She didn't want to be anywhere near him—and she didn't particularly want to explore her reasons for that. Or how they might have changed since she'd walked into that chapel what felt like a lifetime ago. "A hotel or guest room, it's all the same to me."

And she knew, somehow, that just then they were both standing on the edge of that same precipice. They were both being rocked by the same wind, making their footing unsteady.

Just as she knew that left to his own devices, Lionel would jump.

Geraldine had no idea what part of her it was that rather thought she would like to do the same.

The night seemed closer. The candles danced. He had called her beautiful, and more, she thought he meant it.

She had never wanted to be beautiful before. She wasn't sure she liked how much she wanted it now.

Particularly here. With this man, of all men.

But every single buttery-hot sensation that moved through her then, she told herself harshly, was a betrayal. The way her breath caught. The sweet weight of her breasts, the way they moved against the soft fabric of her dress each time she breathed. That sparkling, melting part of her, deep in her belly and high between her legs.

She was betraying Seanna. And she hated herself for it.

Or she should.

Geraldine took one step back, then another. And she did her best to arrange her features into something scornful.

"I trust you will not make this difficult," she said, as sharply as she could.

And then, as she watched, his stern, stone face changed.

Because Lionel Asensio smiled.

In a way that made everything inside of her begin to burn, that humming nearly breaking out through her skin.

"Run along, my little innocent," he told her, every inch of him a wolf. Every beautiful, decidedly male inch. "And sleep well. There will be time enough for difficulties in the days to come. This I promise you, Geraldine."

And later, she would be ashamed that she did not turn and saunter away, effortless and unbothered.

But just then, with that particular gleam in his dark gaze making her body feel something like feverish, Geraldine did the only thing she could.

She kicked off her pointless shoes and ran.

CHAPTER SIX

LIONEL HAD SPENT the day immersed in the usual concerns of his various business enterprises, but he was uncomfortably aware that his attention kept wandering. When his attention was normally fixed and unshakable.

Worse, he found his mind returning again and again to last night.

To that moment when he had first seen Geraldine no longer hiding her beauty but honoring it. Making it clear that she was pure diamond, straight through.

Or later, when he had found himself more nearly undone by a single conversation with her than he had been in whole relationships with others.

And he was not sure that he would ever get over the sight of her in bare feet, racing across the flagstones before she disappeared into his house, her dark hair streaming behind her as she moved.

Making it clear that he was not the only one so close to undone.

His people kept him apprised of his new wife's do-

"One Minute" Survey
You get up to **FOUR books** <u>and</u> a Mystery Gift...

> ABSOLUTELY FREE!

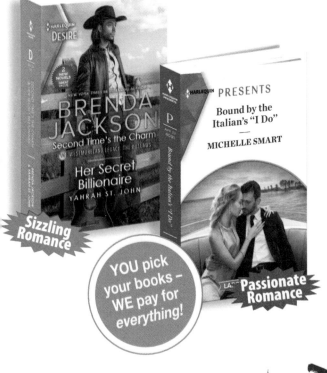

Sizzling Romance

Passionate Romance

YOU pick your books – WE pay for everything!

See inside for details.

YOU pick your books –
WE pay for everything.

You get up to FOUR new books and a Mystery Gift...
absolutely FREE!

Total retail value: Over $20!

Dear Reader,

Your opinions are important to us. So if you'll participate in our fast and free "One Minute" Survey, YOU can pick up to four wonderful books that WE pay for when you try the Harlequin Reader Service!

As a leading publisher of women's fiction, we'd love to hear from you. That's why we promise to reward you for completing our survey.

IMPORTANT: Please complete the survey and return it. We'll send your Free Books and a Free Mystery Gift right away. And we pay for shipping and handling too! *We pay for EVERYTHING!*

Try **Harlequin® Desire** and get 2 books featuring the worlds of the American elite with juicy plot twists, delicious sensuality and intriguing scandal.

Try **Harlequin Presents® Larger-Print** and get 2 books featuring the glamorous lives of royals and billionaires in a world of exotic locations, where passion knows no bounds.

Or TRY BOTH!

Thank you again for participating in our "One Minute" Survey. It really takes just a minute (or less) to complete the survey... and your free books and gift will be well worth it!

If you continue with your subscription, you can look forward to curated monthly shipments of brand-new books from your selected series, always at a discount off the cover price! Plus you can cancel any time. So don't miss out, return your One Minute Survey today to get your Free books.

Pam Powers

"One Minute" Survey

GET YOUR FREE BOOKS AND A FREE GIFT!

✓ Complete this Survey ✓ Return this survey

▶ DETACH AND MAIL CARD TODAY! ▶

1 Do you try to find time to read every day?

☐ YES ☐ NO

2 Do you prefer stories with happy endings?

☐ YES ☐ NO

3 Do you enjoy having books delivered to your home?

☐ YES ☐ NO

4 Do you share your favorite books with friends?

☐ YES ☐ NO

YES! I have completed the above "One Minute" Survey. Please send me my Free Books and a Free Mystery Gift (worth over \$20 retail). I understand that I am under no obligation to buy anything, as explained on the back of this card.

☐ **Harlequin Desire®**
225/326 CTI GRTQ

☐ **Harlequin® Presents Larger-Print**
176/376 CTI GRTQ

☐ **BOTH**
225/326 & 176/376
CTI G294

FIRST NAME

LAST NAME

ADDRESS

APT.#

CITY

STATE/PROV.

ZIP/POSTAL CODE

EMAIL ☐ Please check this box if you would like to receive newsletters and promotional emails from Harlequin Enterprises ULC and its affiliates. You can unsubscribe anytime.

Your Privacy—Your information is being collected by Harlequin Enterprises ULC, operating as Harlequin Reader Service. For a complete summary of the information we collect, how we use this information and to whom it is disclosed, please visit our privacy notice located at https://corporate.harlequin.com/privacy-notice. From time to time we may also exchange your personal information with reputable third parties. If you wish to opt out of this sharing of your personal information, please visit www.readerservice.com/consumerschoice or call 1-800-873-8635. Notice to California Residents—Under California law, you have specific rights to control and access your data. For more information on these rights and how to exercise them, visit https:// corporate.harlequin.com/california-privacy.

© 2023 HARLEQUIN ENTERPRISES ULC
™ and ® are trademarks owned by Harlequin Enterprises ULC. Printed in the U.S.A.

HD/HP-1123-OM_123ST

◆ HARLEQUIN® Reader Service —Here's how it works:

Accepting your 2 free books and free gift (gift valued at approximately $10.00 retail) places you under no obligation to buy anything. You may keep the books and gift and return the shipping statement marked "cancel." If you do not cancel, approximately one month later we'll send you more books from the series you have chosen, and bill you at our low, subscribers-only discount price. Harlequin Presents® Larger-Print books consist of 6 books each month and cost $6.30 each in the U.S. or $6.49 each in Canada, a savings of at least 10% off the cover price. Harlequin Desire® books consist of 3 books (2in1 editions) each month and cost $7.83 each in the U.S. or $8.43 each in Canada, a savings of at least 12% off the cover price. It's quite a bargain! Shipping and handling is just 50¢ per book in the U.S. and $1.25 per book in Canada*. You may return any shipment at our expense and cancel at any time by contacting customer service — or you may continue to receive monthly shipments at our low, subscribers-only discount price plus shipping and handling.

▲ If offer card is missing write to: Harlequin Reader Service, P.O. Box 1341, Buffalo, NY 14240-8531 or visit www.ReaderService.com ▲

BUSINESS REPLY MAIL
FIRST-CLASS MAIL   PERMIT NO. 717   BUFFALO, NY

POSTAGE WILL BE PAID BY ADDRESSEE

HARLEQUIN READER SERVICE
PO BOX 1341
BUFFALO NY 14240-8571

NO POSTAGE
NECESSARY
IF MAILED
IN THE
UNITED STATES

ings throughout the day. She had woken late and had seemed disgruntled, according to the maids, because she had claimed—repeatedly—that she never slept like that, so deeply and so long. She seemed suspicious of the breakfast brought to her in her room, an Andalusian staple of olive oil pressed here at the estate on toast made from freshly baked bread, with a pinch of salt and *jamón serrano*. Even when encouraged to take it out on one of the terraces off her rooms that overlooked the Asensio state, the fields gleaming in the bright fall sun, she had seemed out of sorts until she'd had a fair bit of the *café con leche* that was typical for a Spanish breakfast.

"Perhaps," the maid who brought him this information had theorized, "she is suffering from the jet lag."

"Perhaps," Lionel had said, as if he agreed.

When he was not certain he did.

After her breakfast, his people had laid out dressing options for her—another thing not taken in entirely good grace, according to reports—and then Geraldine had taken herself on a self-guided tour of his home. She had lingered anywhere there was a book, running her fingers down the spines and leafing through the pages. And then she had spent hours in his library, where she had been served a traditional lunch running the gamut from breads and cured meats to gazpacho to a hearty stew and a green salad, with coffee to finish.

She had eaten heartily, then returned to her exploration of his books. And she had not been exactly thrilled when the team of stylists had taken her in hand again, but nor had she objected outright.

All of these things were reported to him, one by one, and with many colorful asides about the new mistress of the house—a term Lionel had not used and was not at all sure he planned to approve—so perhaps it was not very surprising that Lionel could not quite focus the way he would like.

And that evening Lionel found himself waiting for this woman he had married with every expectation of thinking little of her again. He stood ready in the entry hall of his own home so that he might take her hand and lead her into the great celebration that was the entire point of this farce. Because for as long as he had known her—and so therefore, as long as he had been alive—Lionel's iconic and widely revered grandmother had never done anything by half.

Her eightieth birthday party, meticulously plotted out and entirely conceived by Doña Eugenia herself, was certainly no exception to this rule. Lionel had assumed that he would approach this landmark feeling quite pleased with himself, given the trouble he had gone to for the occasion. Collecting a wife as ordered and all.

Yet celebrating the woman who had been the only family he had, and long after she was the only family he acknowledged, was the furthest thing from his mind tonight.

Because Geraldine appeared at the top of the stairs and Lionel could think of nothing and no one else.

For a full moment he was not certain that he was capable of speech. Perhaps it was a great many moments, he would never know. He made an immediate mental note to give all the staff who'd worked with her tonight a hefty raise for their trouble.

Because he was certain, at a glance, that she might very well set the whole of Andalusia alight.

For they had dressed her in a column of flame. Once again, the dress was a love letter to that figure of hers, from her wide hips to her tiny waist to the aching fullness of her breasts. Geraldine, who had looked like a piece of furniture in that chapel yesterday, was today nothing short of a dream come true.

A dream Lionel had not permitted himself to indulge in the night before, but there was nothing to be done about it now. Tonight she was pure sex on two feet.

Yet all he could think was that she was his.

His.

He watched as Geraldine made her way toward him, her green eyes wary, betraying her nerves as she fussed with the dress with every step she took in another pair of shoes that made her legs look like a fantasy come true.

"The more you fidget, the more you call attention to how uncomfortable you are," Lionel said, aware that he sounded not quite himself. It was that or swing her up into his arms, carry her to his bed, and hope his grandmother understood some weeks from now when he emerged, finally sated.

This was likely the first moment in his entire life that Lionel wasn't sure he cared what his grandmother thought at all.

And that was shocking enough that it cleared his head. A little.

Geraldine, naturally, took that opportunity to glare at him, but that hit differently when she was dressed like this. When her beauty was in no way hidden. "I'm not uncomfortable and I don't fidget. I'm nearsighted and I can't see as well as I would like, but they wouldn't let me wear my glasses after I pointed out that this dress is hardly appropriate for an eighty-year-old woman's birthday party."

Lionel moved toward her, then pulled her arm through his. It was an old, courtly sort of gesture, and it sat in him oddly. As if it carried some weight beyond simple expediency.

As if it mattered. Or she did.

He could not allow such thoughts to derail him. "As you will see when you meet my grandmother, *appropriateness* is not a concern. She would be the first to tell you that the only thing that matters in terms of a woman's attire is how glorious she feels while wearing the items in question. And if it can cause a head or two to turn, all the better."

"I think you're brushing past the fact that your people confiscated my glasses a little too quickly."

"You do not need to see," he told her. "Hold on to me and you will be fine."

She scowled at him. "That is not remotely comforting. I think you know that."

Instead of answering her, Lionel led her outside to the waiting Range Rover. Because it was a short walk over the fields to the main house, but tonight he had decided it made sense to take the drive that looped around the long way. Not so much to make certain that they would make an entrance, though he knew all eyes would be on them nonetheless, but also so that his brand-new wife could walk more easily in those shoes that made her legs look as if they would wrap around a man's back all too easily.

"You walk well in those heels," he said as they settled into the back of the vehicle.

Geraldine sighed. "I was a teenage girl once upon a time. I learned how to walk in all kinds of ridiculous shoes. The fact that I *can* walk in them doesn't mean I *want* to walk in them, but I was told in no uncertain terms that I was never going to see *my* shoes again."

"You are welcome," Lionel said, trying to sound more severe than he actually was. "They were an offense against all that is stylish."

And then he consulted the usual flood of messages on his mobile rather than chase up the things he heard her mutter, not quite beneath her breath. But he did not read a word. He was much too busy questioning why it was this woman who should have been overawed by him, yet was not, amused him.

He was not easily amused.

And was less amused by the moment as he wondered why Geraldine, of all women, should bring this out in him.

Moreover, he had not expected to get caught in traffic with half of Spain on the drive to the main house. Inching along meant he was stuck in this confined space with Geraldine, who he knew he could not touch.

Not now. Not *yet*. Not when she had been carefully crafted tonight to appeal to his grandmother as well as wow the crowd.

Lionel found to his surprise that he appeared to be ill-suited to this notion of *waiting* for the things he wanted. He assured himself that this was only because he had been planning to present a wife at this party since his grandmother had decreed she would be throwing it, some eighteen months ago.

It was this situation, he told himself. It wasn't *this woman*.

But he was happier than he thought he ought to be to get out of the Range Rover, all the same.

"There are so many people here," Geraldine said as they walked inside with the gathering crowd. She seemed to have left her scowls and glares back at his house, and Lionel knew he should have been grateful for that. Yet, oddly enough, he was not. As if he liked her unpredictable. "I suppose that makes sense.

Your grandmother must have met a great many in all her years."

"People have been invited to come and pay their respects whether they have met her or not," Lionel told her as they made it through the entryway and were caught up almost at once in the music and the chatter as the flood of guests were directed into the great ballroom. This house had been a part of the court of some-or-other duke who had once claimed these lands, but had then lost them.

Geraldine did not drop his arm as they wound their way through the throngs of well-wishers, and Lionel decided that was a victory of its own. She held on to him, but her eyes could not seem to stay in one place—and made him wonder exactly how blind she really was, hiding behind her glasses. Because tonight her gaze moved from well-known cinema stars to recognizably famous pieces of art on the walls, then seemed to widen at the quiet, understated magnificence of this place that had been the seat of his family for generations.

Despite himself and all the many ways he knew he really needed to treat this like the business venture it was, Lionel found that Geraldine made him... protective. Of her. Because she wasn't the Cartwright heiress—even now happy off in the desert with the man who had claimed her yesterday, according to all reports, and more power to her—who had cut her teeth on parties like this one. *She* had moved in the sorts of circles that would have prepared her for nights like this, like it or not.

Not so Geraldine.

But his many assistants had done their jobs well, and Lionel had been presented with files stuffed full of all the details anyone could ever want about his new wife the night before. Long after she'd run from him, he had sipped at his brandy from Jerez there in his library where he often spent his evenings, and read everything there was to know about Geraldine Gertrude Casey.

Geraldine *Asensio* he corrected himself.

The files his people had compiled proved that she was exactly who she seemed to be, and there was something about that. It seemed to tug at him. It made his throat need clearing.

For the wife of the heir to the Asensio empire had been raised by two schoolteachers outside Minneapolis, which Lionel knew vaguely from his time at Harvard was somewhere in the American Midwest. He'd had to look it up on a map. Geraldine was an only child. She had done exceedingly well at school and had gone to Chicago for college, but had returned home to get her degree in library science, and then, later, her job.

She was enormously well-suited to that life, he thought.

Tonight, he felt very much as if was leading a lamb to the slaughter.

Though he supposed that the saving grace was

how little Geraldine seemed to notice or care that she was the object of so much speculation that Lionel could actually *feel* the weight of so many stares as they walked through the ballroom.

Because it was known far and wide that even when Lionel was indulging in one of his relationships, he never brought a woman here. Not to this house.

Not when his grandmother was in residence.

He could see members of the Spanish nobility, who he would never quite call *friends*, gossiping behind their hands as he walked Geraldine through the crowd. He saw the same assessment on the faces of politicians and celebrities. Yet he did not stop. He did not want to let anyone get their hooks into her.

Even though he knew that if anyone could handle herself, even in a place like this that better resembled a lion's den tonight, it was Geraldine.

Lionel did not stop no matter who caught his eye or waved him over. He kept going until he achieved his target.

"Behold," he intoned, with all due deference, inclining his head. "May I present *la ilustrísima* señora Doña Eugenia Lourdes Rosario Asensio." Geraldine inclined her head the way everyone else did when they approached his grandmother. "Grandmother, this is my Geraldine."

Geraldine blinked in astonishment at last, but Lionel thought that had more to do with the *my Geral-*

dine than anything else. She looked up at him for a beat too long, then followed his gaze.

To his grandmother, who sat in all her considerable state in what might as well have been a throne, set up on a dais at the far end of the room so she might cast an eye wherever she liked over the proceedings and see everything she would not if she was on the ground.

I am a tiny woman, she had told Lionel on one of their typical morning walks.

Only in physical stature, he had replied loyally.

She had tutted at him. *Obviously,* nene, she had said reproachfully. *I am otherwise grander than the sky, and don't you forget it.*

His *abuelita* sat so that everyone who came to greet her was slightly below her eye level, like the queen she had always been in Lionel's estimation.

She had always been breathtaking, though she had long since left the sloe-eyed, mysteriously beautiful girl she'd been behind—the one who still claimed pride of place in a great many portraits painted by modern masters all over this house. But Doña Eugenia was not one to cling to her lost youth, freezing her brow or injecting questionable substances into her skin. She had settled into her years with grace and elegance and tonight her snow-white hair was arranged about her face in such a way as to suggest that she might just be wearing a crown. She wore a set of priceless emeralds around her neck, each the size of a small fist. And she clasped a cane before her that was topped by the bejeweled head of the serpent, with rubies for eyes.

Because, she had told Lionel when she'd showed the cane to him last week, *I do not wish to be too approachable.*

Even at your own party? he had asked.

Especially at my own party" she had declared.

"She's absolutely magnificent," Geraldine breathed.

No talk about how ferocious his grandmother was. No hint of intimidation.

Deep inside, Lionel felt something kick at him, hard.

But his grandmother was watching. She lifted one aristocratic finger and beckoned him close.

"I hope you're ready," Lionel murmured to Geraldine.

Then he brought forth the woman he had married to meet the only woman he had ever loved. And felt something twist in him that he could not possibly have explained if asked. As if this, here, was his true wedding. As if this was the only ceremony that mattered.

His grandmother waved the rest of her admirers away. They melted away at her command, because she wasn't the sort of woman that anyone dared disobey. As she was the first to say, she had been less formidable in her youth. *But the true power in this world is outliving everybody,* she liked to say with a laugh.

"Abuelita," Lionel said as he stepped up onto the dais and brought Geraldine with him, "I am certain that you have never been more beautiful than you are tonight."

"Whereas you used to be far better at flattery," his salty grandmother responded in her usual crisp manner, presenting her one cheek to be kissed, then the other.

"May I present to you the woman that I have made my wife," Lionel said, and in English. "Geraldine Gertrude Casey, who did me the great honor of taking my name only yesterday at Lake Como."

As he spoke, Geraldine stood beside him. She was not exactly relaxed, but she did not appear overly intense, either. This allowed him to pay closer attention to his grandmother. He watched different emotions chase across her usually inscrutable face. Shock. The faintest hint of temper. Then, at last, consideration.

"Have I already gone to meet my maker?" she asked Lionel. In Spanish, because she could not be told or led. "Is there reason that my only grandson saw fit to marry himself off outside of my presence? What can you be playing at, I wonder?"

"We were swept away by passion," Lionel told her, expressionless. "It was necessary that we marry as quickly as possible."

"Is that so?"

His grandmother turned that lively dark gaze of hers to Geraldine, and studied her for a long moment. And Lionel did not know if Geraldine realized how critical it was that the way she appeared in this moment was nothing short of perfection. But he did.

"There are only two things that cause anyone to rush to an altar, as far as I am aware," Doña Eugenia said, this time in perfectly crisp English. "One is a feverish desire for consummation. The other is the fear of illegitimacy. And which was this clandestine ceremony, might I ask?"

Lionel could see the way his grandmother's gaze still moved all over Geraldine, no doubt cataloging flaws at every turn. She might have been the kindest and approachable of his family members. She might always have been his favorite.

This did not mean she was cuddly.

He should have prepared his new wife better for this. Had he spent less time trying his best not to think too much about her, he might have.

But next to him, Geraldine smiled. "There are some men who only value something if they are required to work for it," she told his grandmother, in a voice that somehow managed to be respectful and amused at once.

And then, as Lionel stood there feeling surplus to requirements for what was likely the first time in his life, the two women gazed at each other for a long moment. Then another one, as the band played old standards and the better part of fashionable Spain tried to eavesdrop without appearing to do so.

Until, to Lionel's great astonishment, his grandmother laughed. "Fair enough," she said, and did not precisely incline her head to Geraldine, though the notion seemed to hang between them anyway. Then she shifted her gaze to Lionel. "Now that you are here, the dancing can begin at last. Had I known you would go to such lengths to exclude me from your wedding ceremony, I might not have gone to the trouble of waiting for you."

"*Abuelita.* Come now. You know as well as I do that you no longer wish to travel. How many times have you told me that the world must come to you?" He indicated the still-growing crowd behind them. "And so they have."

"You are saying it was your new wife's choice to exclude me?" But she was still smiling, if more at Geraldine than Lionel. "How ungallant."

"I could have invited you. But I thought you might prefer it if I arrived here at the party with the best present you could possibly wish for." He nodded at Geraldine. "The Asensio line, assured at last."

"You will forgive me if I wait a bit longer to applaud you for acquitting yourself of those responsibilities, *nene*," his grandmother said dryly. "It isn't only the marrying that matters to the bloodline, as well you know."

Lionel sighed. "I have had a wife for only slightly more than twenty-four hours. Perhaps we could have a slight grace period before we decorate the nursery."

"What I can give you is the first dance," his grandmother told him instead, and rapped her cane against the floor.

Across the room, the musicians stopped playing. Then started again as the dance floor cleared.

And Lionel had absolutely no choice but to take Geraldine's hand in his. He bowed to his grandmother, as much a mockery of something genteel as anything else, but it made her laugh.

He had known it would.

Then he pulled his wife with him, off the dais and out into the center the dance floor. Once there, he pulled Geraldine into his arms and did not care for the sensation of something like *relief* that enveloped him. Nor did he wish to pursue it, or think what it might mean.

He thought instead of the fact that, even in those heels of hers, he was still taller than her in a way he liked. And in a way she liked too, if that shine in her green gaze was any indication. Lionel wrapped one hand around hers, then slid his other hand down, anchoring it in the small of her back.

"Do you know how to dance?" he asked her, aware of that husky note in his voice, but he did not wish to consider that too closely, either.

A kind of humor flitted through her eyes, making them gleam like emeralds all their own. "Not a single step."

"Then I suggest you simply let go and let me lead." He tipped his head slightly to one side. "Do you think this is something you can manage?"

And he understood that he'd said that precisely so that it would light that fire of battle in her gaze.

"That will depend on how good you are at leading, I would imagine," she clipped back at him.

Lionel let himself smile. Then he pulled her closer, and began.

And with every step, the room around them retreated further and further away.

He could tell she was inexperienced, but she kept her gaze on his. And he found her fluid and lithe as they moved through the steps of the dance and knew it could only be because, somehow, the chemistry that he had felt last night had been no mirage. No attempt to make sense of the ruin of his plans, but a very real thread pulling them both together.

Because she might claim that he was untrustworthy, a despoiler of young girls, the kind of man who would toss not only a woman aside, but any baby she carried besides.

But her body told a different story.

And every time they turned, every time they moved, all Lionel could think was, *mine.*

Mine.

One number ended and another began, but Lionel did not let her go. Nor did he release her for the next song, or the one after that.

It was not until he heard that same rapping of his grandmother's cane that he finally stepped back and allowed space he didn't want between him and Geraldine.

Geraldine, who looked flushed and full of wonder. Geraldine, who was without question the most beautiful woman he had ever beheld. Especially when she looked at him this way, as if it was the sight of him alone that set her alight.

Geraldine, who had married him and who he intended to make his wife in every possible way, no matter what it cost him.

But first there was his grandmother, and this party.

Lionel brought her over to his grandmother again, and this time, there was a different sort of look in the canny old woman's eyes.

"I have decided I like you," she told Geraldine. "What have you to say to that?"

"I'm delighted," Geraldine replied, cheerfully enough. "But I cannot think it is me you like, as you don't know me at all. I must warn you, I can be a handful."

"That's all for the best," his grandmother said airily. She leaned forward, her hands propped up on that cane. "Lionel is a good man, but he has been raised to consider himself above all others."

"What man has not?" asked Geraldine.

And Lionel could not say that he particular cared for the way Geraldine and his grandmother both laughed at that, a wealth of understanding between them.

"I have always told him that I require an innocent," the older woman continued, her gaze moving from Geraldine to Lionel, then back again. Looking for evidence, Lionel rather thought. "And this is not simply because I am an ancient relic. It is because, in the fullness of time, I believe that a man is more likely to treasure something he knows has always and ever been his. They are so possessive, you see."

"I'm standing right here," Lionel reminded her.

Geraldine didn't even look at him. "Are they? That does not seem to be a universal experience. Besides, pledging one's troth to another until death seems to cover all the same bases without putting the weight of an entire marriage on one poor bride's virginity."

"My dear girl," his grandmother said mildly, though her gaze was intent, "I hate to be the bearer of bad news. But I think you will find that it is often the wife who carries the weight of a marriage, like it or not. Virginity has nothing to do with it."

"Does anyone possess enough purity to please the nearest priest?" Geraldine asked, lightly enough. "I'm not sure that's something to aspire to, if I'm honest."

Doña Eugenia leaned forward, then. "Purity is not for priests. Priests are but men. It is for the husbands who proclaim that they care little about such things, only to find themselves awake in the middle of the night, fretting over situations that can never be changed. You understand."

Geraldine looked as if she might. Lionel wished that he did—because all that made him do was replay what he knew of his grandparents' chilly marriage, wondering how it had ended up that way.

Another topic he did not care to explore.

"In the absence of a bloodstained sheet to wave about in front of the villagers," Geraldine said with what Lionel found to be admirable calm in the face of such provocation, "I suppose you will simply have to take my word for it that if your grandson is awake in the middle of the night, wracked with concern over my past, I will be more than happy to wake up and talk him through it."

Lionel fully expected his grandmother to take issue with that in the way she took issue with so much else, always. But once again, she surprised him. Because all she did was look at Geraldine for a long while, then laugh yet again.

"Marvelous," she said. "I wish you both every happiness in the world." And when Lionel found himself gazing back at her, in something like shock, she waved her hand toward the dance floor again. "Dance, *nene*. For soon enough, you will be sitting where I am and wishing that you had. While you still could."

And once again, Lionel obeyed her.

"I think that went well," Geraldine said as he took her in his arms again. "Though I suppose I wouldn't know."

"You would know," Lionel assured her.

But he did not wish to talk about his grandmother any longer.

Because Geraldine was in his arms, and he was certain that everyone who looked at them believed that they had spent many long, sleepless nights in his bed. How else could they move together the way they did, with such ease and grace?

When only the two of them knew the truth. That they had barely kissed.

Lionel spun her around and around. In between dances, when he had to put space between them or cause a scene, he took her about the room, on his arm. He introduced her to all of these bright and shining creatures he considered friends—though he would cut them all off in an instant if they tried to sharpen their favorite little knives against his bride.

And it was much, much later, so late that there were already the hints of the new day in the sky, when they finally made it back down to his house. He helped her from the car and they walked inside to find everything hushed and the lights down low.

Lionel was not certain that he could bear this. Or perhaps it was that he did not want to. That he did not know how anyone could.

"Tell me," he urged her in a low voice as he stood there, much closer to her than was necessary, now they were alone. And not dancing. Not in any sense of the term. "Tell me what you want, Geraldine."

Because he already knew what he wanted. He already knew exactly how he wished to kiss her first. How he longed to slide his hands all over the marvelous hourglass of her body. How he wanted to kneel somewhere, and this would do, so he might get his mouth between her legs at last.

Lionel already knew, beyond any doubt, exactly how he wished to learn her.

She was even more beautiful here, in this soft

light. Or perhaps because he could hear the way she caught her breath, here in the space between them. Or because he alone could see the way her green eyes gleamed with a light he considered his own now, and her cheeks flushed, pinker by the second.

He reached over and traced a little bit of that flush with his fingers, marveling at the warm satin of her skin. And the way she quivered there before him as if the way that ran through him, electric and intense, was lighting her up inside, too.

"Tell me, *mi querida esposa*," he whispered, there the barest millimeter away from those lips of hers that haunted him already. "My Geraldine, only tell me what it is you want and I will make it yours."

Her eyes fluttered closed. She swayed on those impossible heels of hers.

And Lionel could not recall ever wanting anything the way he wanted this. The way he wanted *her*, so much that he was shoving aside the alarms that rang inside him, warning him that he was much too close to breaking each and every one of his own rules—

"I only want one thing, Lionel," she whispered, and for a moment, she pressed her cheek into his hand. He felt it like fire, but then she straightened. And Geraldine's green eyes were distressingly clear when she caught his gaze again. "A paternity test for Jules. Tonight."

CHAPTER SEVEN

GERALDINE WOULD NEVER know how she managed to get those words out, when they weren't at all what she wanted to say. They were what she *should* say, and so she had, but then she'd wished that somehow she could claw them back from where they hung in the air between them—

It was the look on Lionel's face, she thought. It was that expression of his, as close to shock and betrayal as she imagined a man like him ever got.

There was only an instant of it. Just that one little instant—but then he stepped away, his dark gaze shuttering.

And when he looked at her again, it was as if he had never touched her at all.

She told herself that was a good thing.

Especially when she woke up, late again, to find her mother being ushered into her bedroom with the baby in her arms.

The baby. *Her* baby. Her Jules. Geraldine was up before she knew it, crossing the floor of the bedchamber so she could take the laughing, cooing child into her arms. Then cover her sweet, beloved, damp little face with kisses.

"Geraldine Gertrude," her mother said in a voice so low and so appalled that it made Geraldine flinch. "What have you *done*?"

"What I must," Geraldine replied over the baby's head, seriously enough.

But it was only when she saw her mother's gaze widen, then focus on the rumpled bed behind her that she understood what her mother thought was going on here.

"I didn't sleep with the man we think is Jules's *father*," she said, with perhaps more righteous indignation than was strictly called for. Given she had kissed the man. And danced with him. And run from him two nights in a row, in one way or another. Still, she stood straighter and stared her mother straight in the eyes. "What do you take me for?"

"I don't like any of this," her mother said, which wasn't really an answer. "These aren't how regular people behave. All this gallivanting about from *Italy* to *Spain* on a lark. I don't like it."

"You used to tell me that life wasn't worth living without a few adventures thrown in to spice it up," Geraldine reminded her. "When did that change?"

Her mother blinked, and then, just for a moment, looked a little more like the woman who had always told her only daughter that the only limits she should ever set were the ones she chose, not ones that anyone else tried to press upon her.

"That was before," Lorna Casey said quietly. Her mother held her gaze, a bit hard. "I couldn't lose you the way we lost Seanna, Geraldine. I couldn't cope."

And hours later, Geraldine was still replaying that in her head.

It was long after the fleet of doctors came in, made the baby laugh, and ran their little tests. Her summons had come a mere quarter of an hour earlier in the form of her phalanx of stylists. They had all come whirling into the room, ignoring her mother and insisting that Geraldine get dressed according to their specifications.

Something she couldn't begin to explain to her mother, who had been wearing the same pair of jeans for the past thirty years, and so didn't try.

Geraldine went out of her way to avoid her mother's eyes when she left at last, dressed in what she suspected was supposed to pass for a casual outfit in this place. The sort of high-waisted, wide-leg trousers that she had only seen in magazines, though she had to admit that they felt like a caress against her legs as she walked. With a tight-fitting, high-necked sleeveless blouse that her favorite stylist, the man called Angel, had told her was for *that little kick of clever* to go along with *the classically chic*.

She wasn't thinking about clever or chic when she walked into the library to find Lionel waiting for her. His grandmother was there too, wearing an outfit not dissimilar to the one Geraldine was sporting, though Doña Eugenia was bedecked in far more gems and fine jewels.

What she couldn't decide was when or why, over the past two nights, she had become the sort of person who noticed such things.

"Your cousin's baby is a lovely little thing," Lionel said, every word measured. He tapped a set of papers sitting before him, and Geraldine was unreasonably pleased that she'd managed to keep her glasses for this. Because it felt like a bit of armor as she waited, her stomach heavy with what she refused to call *dread.* "But she is not mine. As I told you."

And Geraldine would never know what kept her from reacting to that news the way she wanted. Once his words arranged themselves into some kind of sense inside her. Once she fully understood what they meant.

Once she realized that what she felt was a kind of bone-deep, systemic relief that she had no intention of acknowledging, much less analyzing.

Just as she had no intention of collapsing into the nearest chair, either. Because it was no one's business but hers what the state of her knees were, so shivery beneath her just then.

"But how do I know that I can believe what you're telling me?" she made herself ask. "I'm certain that all those doctors that you managed to get to turn up here would happily say anything you want them to say."

"I had the very same thought," Lionel's grandmother said then, with a thump of her cane against the floor. And when Lionel raised a brow in her direction, she only smiled. "I love my grandson, dear. But it has not escaped my notice that he, regrettably, is a man. And even the best of them can act a fool. I had my personal doctor run the test again. But I am afraid it came back with same answer. And that is a pity. Because I quite fancy myself as a doting grandparent."

"Doting?" Lionel queried. "Are you certain that is within your capabilities, *Abuelita?*"

She said something in Spanish that made Lionel smile, then looked back at Geraldine. "Lionel tells me that you both agreed to take a honeymoon sometime in the future, but I must insist that you reconsider. It is my belief that the true beating heart of a marriage can only be heard at first during the honeymoon. I have always said so."

"You have never said such a thing in all your days," Lionel said darkly.

His grandmother waved her hand languidly. "And yet I know I am right."

"*That* you have said a great many times."

As if she had only needed confirmation from herself, and ignoring her grandson, the old woman angled herself up from the chair where she sat—with an agility that Geraldine found questionable. It was as if the cane was for show.

"It is settled. I shall find the finest nannies and

nurses in the whole of Spain to make certain the child wants for nothing. And you and this grandson of mine will do what all newlyweds must do in the perfect privacy you deserve." Doña Eugenia shifted her gaze to Lionel, an obvious challenge even from where Geraldine stood. "The entire Asensio empire will not crumble without you over the course of a single little month, *nene*. Believe me."

"A month is entirely too long," Lionel said, certain tightness in his voice then. "The world is not as slow as you might recall it."

"Said no besotted new groom ever," replied his grandmother. And then matched his lifted brow with her own.

The family resemblance was astonishing, Geraldine thought. But she was glad they were too busy glaring at each other to pay any attention to what she was or wasn't doing. Currently, she was still trying not to *shake*. With that same relief coursing through her like its own kind of heat.

Lionel wasn't the father. *He wasn't the father.*

It took her a moment to realize it when they stopped staring each other down and turned to her instead.

"This is such a kind offer," she made herself say, somehow keeping her voice even. "But my mother is here."

She shrugged, as if her mother required a chaperone when Lorna Casey was nothing if not a great fan of her own company. Anywhere and everywhere.

"Nonsense," said Doña Eugenia grandly. "I feel certain that I can entertain your mother, my girl. My company has enchanted no less than kings and presidents in my day. I flatter myself that I can make anyone at all feel at home, should I wish it."

And then, as if she was considering being affronted, she swept from the room. Leaving Geraldine face-to-face with Lionel at last. This time, feeling dizzy for more than one reason.

Geraldine thought he might gloat, then. But all he did was slide the papers toward the edge of the table where he stood, then tap them again, his gaze an intensity that made her want to shake all the more.

"What I need you to know," he said, very intently, "is that what I have told you is true. Your cousin was too young for me. She was not well. But even if, somehow, those things had escaped me, I do not walk away from my responsibilities. I never have and I never will. Do we understand each other now, you and I?"

And Geraldine had the strangest urge to give in to the sob that seemed to be gathering there, right behind her ribs. Not because he had been telling her the truth. Not even because she needed to start the search for Jules's paternity all over again.

But because he wasn't looking at her the way he had been last night, with all of that longing and desire, and that molten gleam in his dark gaze.

The loss of it felt like more grief than she could bear.

"Lionel..." she began, but something bright and

hot seemed to arc between them, there in the library with only the books as witness.

"I like hearing my name in your mouth," he told her, dark as sin. "I intend to hear it often over the next month."

She swallowed, hard. "Because, naturally, you will not be telling your grandmother *no*."

His eyes were so dark and rich that it was as if she could feel them inside her. "I will not."

She felt that bright heat between them again, and wanted nothing more than to reach out and touch it. To close the distance between them, and—

And.

That was the trouble. There was so much on the other side of the word *and*.

Particularly because, she couldn't help but think, she didn't have to tear herself apart for harboring all these strangely overwhelming *feelings* for a man who'd abandoned her cousin.

"I suppose I'd better go tell my mother she's about to have her very own Spanish vacation," Geraldine said instead of leaning into all that *and*. Even though she was sure that the glint she saw in Lionel's gaze as she backed away from him was laughter. Possibly even mockery. *And, and, and—* She shoved her glasses into place. "With a new best friend to boot."

Then she turned and bolted for her rooms.

But Lorna declined the offer to stay in Spain for all that time. "What would I do?" she asked, shaking her head as she looked out the window at all the rolling hills and vineyards. It was all a far cry from the view out back of Geraldine's childhood home. "Besides, your father needs seeing to."

Geraldine imagined that somewhere in Minnetonka, Patrick Casey sat up straight at that, understanding he was being maligned from all the way across the planet. As he had never been the sort of man who needed his wife to do things for him that he could himself.

And Geraldine did not ask her mother to take Jules. Not only because she knew that her mother wouldn't do it. But because Jules was *hers*, and there was something in that acknowledgment that felt different, now. Because she had spent all this time thinking that finding the man who'd gotten Seanna pregnant meant that maybe, somewhere out there, there was a man who would be interested in stepping up to his responsibilities. Or paying for his disinterest. But it turned out that she still didn't know who that was. And in the meantime, a baby girl needed a parent.

Geraldine had been her mother all along.

Maybe it was time that she accepted that, then, as her own mother stepped away.

"And you married him?" Lorna asked, still not quite looking Geraldine in the eye. As if she feared the answer when she already knew it. "On purpose?"

There were so many things that Geraldine could have said to that, but she didn't. She held Jules. She pressed her lips to the baby's soft, warm head.

"I suppose I did," was all she said.

Her mother let out a sigh that was much too close to a sob.

"Then I will leave you to it," she murmured, as if she was keeping her voice low to hide the crack in it.

But somehow, the pain in that gave Geraldine the strength she hadn't quite understood she needed. *I couldn't lose you the way we lost Seanna, Geraldine,* her mother had said earlier. *I couldn't cope.*

So she left Lorna to fuss with her bag, as if it needed repacking when it plainly did not. Geraldine didn't argue with her. She made her way back out into the hall and down the stairs until she was in the main part of the house. Instead of walking out through the atrium again to find the garden, or out the front door to the grand foyer, she turned in the other direction and started down a different hall.

And she knew at once that she had entered Lionel's domain.

There was a subtle shift in the art on the wall, though it was not until she walked some ways down the hall that she realized the difference. The walls boasted canvases with bold lines and arresting colors while in the main part of the house, the art tended more toward Old Masters and pieces that became a part of the decor as a whole rather than making her want to stop and look more closely.

She didn't stop now, either. But she was aware that she wanted to. And she wasn't surprised that this hall did not lead to a warren of little rooms leading off it like the part of the house she was staying in, but instead opened up into a grand open space that felt both out of place in a house like this and entirely of it.

She understood at once that Lionel had fashioned himself a kind of loft space, here in this ancient place, when she would have expected something far more traditional. She let her gaze move over the exposed beams beneath the glass ceiling, the grand fireplace in one corner, the spare yet comfortable furnishings.

And then, at last, turned to find the man himself sitting on one of the low leather sofas with stacks of documents piled to one side of him, his computer on his lap, and more documents before him on a low, wide coffee table.

"I would have thought you'd have an office for that," Geraldine said without thinking.

As if his office arrangements were the point of any of this. And as if that was what she'd come here to discuss with him.

One of his eyebrows rose, but he did not otherwise react. "I've a great many offices, Geraldine. And when I wish to go to one of them, I do. Other times I prefer to work at home. I know my grandmother thinks otherwise, but the Asensio empire does not exist simply because she thinks it should. It takes work, I am afraid."

His gaze moved from her to the baby she held, and she wasn't sure that she could quite define the look on his face then.

Or maybe it was that she wasn't sure she wanted to.

"My mother would prefer to go home," Geraldine told him. "And to be honest, I think it would be best she did."

"My grandmother is not used to her plans being upended." But Lionel did not sound as if he minded it happening, even so. "Perhaps it will be good for her to remember that the entire world does not revolve around her, despite all indications to the contrary."

Jules began to kick and wave her arms in the air, so Geraldine set her down in the center of the plush, richly colored rug that took over the middle of the big room. She watched the baby for a moment, knowing that it wouldn't be long now before Jules would turn that rocking into crawling, and then, shortly after that, toddling around on her feet.

You should be here for this, she thought, sending a message to her cousin the way she often did, inside.

Geraldine straightened to find that Lionel had stood, too. She moved toward him, telling herself that there was no reason for her heart to be beating like that in her chest. He was only *looking* at her. The baby was *right here*. Surely there was a limit to…whatever might come of this heat she wished she didn't feel.

"I think that I should go with her," Geraldine said, and was suddenly aware that the words she was choosing were like mines. And that the way his dark eyes gleamed meant she needed to watch her step. "I never meant to marry you, as you know. I only did because I thought you might be Jules's father. But you're not, so it seems to me we would be better off annulling the whole thing and going our separate ways."

"But this is impossible," he said softly, but it was the kind of *soft* that made the back of her neck prickle. "Did I not make this clear? My grandmother is to be happy. Your mother does not need to stay here to achieve this. But I am afraid you do."

"I think the fact that she wants us to take a honeymoon can work perfectly," Geraldine argued. "You can simply tell her at the end of the month that it didn't work out between us. That you thought it might, but were mistaken. These things happen all the time."

He shook his head as if he was sad, but she could see his expression. She could tell that he was nothing of the kind.

"These things do not happen here, Geraldine. Asensios do not divorce." He was closer then, and Geraldine felt the oddest sensation inside her. It was as if her heart was beating so hard that it might knock her back and then tip her over at any moment. "Certainly not as long as my grandmother is alive, at any rate."

"You can't possibly be suggesting that we carry on with this farce?" Geraldine was astonished. "For any number of years?"

"I'm not suggesting it." Lionel's voice was still

soft, but the stone in it was unmistakable. "I'm insisting upon it."

Geraldine glanced over at the baby, still gurgling happily to herself as she lay on the floor, kicking out her little legs. Then she looked back at Lionel.

"And if I refuse?"

And later, perhaps, she would think about how strange it was that she had never sounded quite so calm in the whole of her life.

But then, his eyes had never seemed so dark. Or so *inside* her. "You can refuse all you like, *mi querida esposa*. It will change nothing."

She was still so oddly calm. "It will make all of this unpleasant, I would think."

"What if I have another idea?" he asked in that same soft, stone way.

Geraldine watched, feeling almost as if she was in some kind of dream, as he closed that last bit of distance between them. He reached out, running his hands down from her shoulders to grip her upper arms.

Then he pulled her closer to him, as if it was inevitable. As if they had always been destined to be right here, right now, her head tipped back to look up at him and his harshly beautiful face blocking out the sky she should have been able to see above him through the glass ceiling.

It was as if her whole life had been an arrow pointing here, to that place where her pulse beat wildly in her throat.

The place he already knew about, because Lionel leaned down and pressed his mouth directly upon it.

Then, both gently and not gently at all, he scraped his teeth along the surface of her skin.

Just a little.

Just enough.

Because everything she was seemed to *implode*. To melt and then reform again into one great, long, luxuriant shiver. A shimmering sort of comet that shot straight through her from the point of impact, reaching deep between her legs, where it burst apart anew.

She felt him laugh, there against her own body. And it was a low, flammable, glorious thing, scorching her where she stood.

Geraldine had the presence of mind to push him back. And then, more critically, to step away herself. Then keep right on backing up until she could scoop Jules up once more.

"We will remain married no matter what you choose," he told her quietly. And there was a promise there that she desperately wanted to call a threat.

And might have, if she hadn't been chasing fire with more fire herself.

When she had the distinct impression that all of it was the same sort of need and hunger within.

Later that night, long after she put Jules to bed and told his grandmother's staff that she would be doing so every night for as long as she stayed here, she found herself standing out on her own terrace as the night came in.

Missing her mother. Missing her cousin.

Missing the version of herself she'd been before she'd come here, so certain that everything was black-and-white and she could slay any dragon she encountered by force of will alone.

Missing the version of her that wouldn't have understood what she felt right now, because she'd never felt anything like it and—if she'd stayed in Minneapolis—never would have. She had built a life that would never lead to this or anything like it.

And besides, came a wise sort of voice from deep inside her, *you would never have met* him *there.*

Geraldine sighed. And she understood the layout of this house now, so she walked along the terrace until she could see around the corner and into Lionel's wing. And felt everything in her spin and whirl, because he was in there now.

There was no sign of his office work. Just him, sitting on that couch again, this time swirling a drink in one hand.

Looking brooding and implacable and delicious in ways she couldn't entirely admit to herself.

Geraldine told herself that he couldn't see her, because the lights were on where he was and she stood in the dark, but her body knew different. Every hair on her body seemed to be lost in those dances from last night, standing on end and swaying as if his hands were still all over her...

Maybe he couldn't see her, she thought when he shifted, but he knew she was here.

And she let out a breath, though it shook.

The terrible truth was that she wanted him.

Geraldine had never felt anything like this before in her life.

She did not deceive herself. He did not want a divorce, but he certainly didn't want her as his wife in any real way.

That should have been enough to send her packing and looking for escape routes.

But she *wanted* him.

And maybe she could have fought that, but it would necessitate leaving this place and leaving *him* and she wasn't quite sure how she would do that if he didn't allow it. She knew where she was on a map, but all the staff were loyal to him, she spoke only a few words of Spanish, and didn't have private jets at her disposal.

Yet even if she did, where would she go? Back to Minneapolis where she was certain Jules's father was not? If she had to start from scratch in that search, it seemed obvious to her that it would be a lot easier to do here, already in Europe.

If she thought about all that, it almost felt rational.

Geraldine knew that it wasn't.

She knew that the real reason she was even considering this had nothing to do with paternity tests, and everything to do with him. With Lionel himself. With the way they'd danced last night. She had surrendered herself to him, to the music, and it had felt like flying. Yet all the while she had been anchored to the earth and the way his hand pressed against her back. The way the other gripped her hand. The way he looked down at her, all gleaming dark eyes and the hint of a dangerous smile.

Tonight that spot on her neck still pulsed too hard from before. She could still feel the graze of his teeth against her flesh.

Surely, a voice inside her whispered dangerously, *you deserve to feel* something *for once. Maybe more than* something.

And Geraldine had always been distressingly practical. She understood, as she stared out across the Andalusian night into the windows where the most relentlessly masculine man she'd ever beheld sat waiting, that there was far more at risk here than the loss of a few years, her autonomy, or the respect of her family and friends.

There was her heart, already feeling precarious in her chest. Likely because she couldn't seem to separate what she knew intellectually was a physical reaction from her emotional response to the fact that Lionel Asensio was the only man who had ever made her feel like that.

Who had ever made her feel much of anything at all.

A smart woman would rejoice that she *could* feel and then run in the opposite direction, and Geraldine had always prided herself on being smart.

But instead she stood here, on the first night of her official honeymoon with this man she should never have met in the first place.

And she knew herself well enough to know that she'd already decided.

He wanted her. And she wanted to know what that meant. What that was.

What those promises in his dark gaze meant.

She would be his.

Whatever that looked like and for however long this lasted.

And she would worry about picking up the pieces later.

CHAPTER EIGHT

LIONEL LEARNED A GREAT many things about himself in the weeks that followed.

First, that he was not accustomed to delayed gratification. He found this a bit of a surprise, for he considered not being able to wait a deep flaw that he had witnessed entirely too many times from his father and grandfather. He had long considered himself made of sterner stuff.

And yet the fact remained that he was not used to wanting something he could not simply have. Certainly not when it came to women.

Second, and related, was that he found he had never truly experimented with the limits of his self-control before, and certainly not while enjoying such close proximity to the object of his desire.

The truth was, he had never imagined any of this to be a factor. It would not have occurred to him that it could be.

He was Lionel Asensio. He had never known a woman to spend much time in his presence before offering herself to him on the nearest silver platter. Some women did not require an introduction. Most women were drawn to him without him having to do more than…exist.

But Geraldine was like no other woman he had ever encountered.

It was almost as if she did it on purpose—but he knew too well that she did not. That what he saw was who she was, always. For a man who had always considered himself the soul of directness and forthrightness, despite his upbringing, Lionel found it nothing short of confronting that this woman had him beat in both of those areas.

If she didn't also tempt him beyond reason, he wasn't at all sure what he would make of her.

He had insisted that they eat their meals together. He had done so as a counterpoint to her demands when she had agreed to stay here with him for the honeymoon period his grandmother had demanded. All the things Geraldine had insisted upon involved the child. She refused to hand the baby off to nannies entirely. She refused to spend a month—or even a day—apart from little Jules.

A lesser man might have been displeased that he took second place to an infant.

But Lionel found the way she cared for a child that was not even of her own flesh made her seem to glow all the more for him.

And so it was that they sat there every morning in the part of his great room that was set aside for eating, and watched the way the new day moved over the fields beyond.

"I begin to understand the entire purpose of honeymoons," she told him one morning.

"I do not believe you do understand their purpose at all," he replied darkly, because his body understood. Only too well. His body wanted all kinds of things that he would have thought were the whole purpose of a honeymoon, of any description or length.

The kind of things he thought about late into the night, staring up at his ceiling and imagining she was with him…

Yet he was only too aware that this was not at all what Geraldine was talking about.

As she quickly made clear.

"It works no matter what type of marriage you've embarked upon," she said brightly, buttering her toast. "If it's some kind of arranged situation, like the one you had planned to have, well, then. You have a honeymoon to get to know the stranger you married. If it's a love match, you get to deepen your feelings. But really, I do think it's a bit ingenious that once upon a time, someone assumed that what couples needed most of all was to be locked away together if anything was to come of it."

"What was to come of it was a child," Lionel pointed out. "That would be the entire purpose. The phase of the moon to get a new wife pregnant, because that is, of course, the only purpose of a marriage in some eyes."

Geraldine, he had come to realize, was remarkably good at ignoring anything she did not wish to discuss. She only glanced at him today, a simple touch of that maddeningly cool green gaze. "Lucky for you, then, that there is already a child."

As if she didn't understand what he meant when he knew very well that she did.

But she had negotiated more time with Jules than Lionel had expected she would want. He could not recall his own mother insisting that she see to his bedtime. Or that she see him much at all. She had been a shadowy figure in Lionel's life. He had been raised by nannies, nurses, and tutors when his grandmother was unavailable, and had been presented to his father and grandfather infrequently.

Geraldine insisted on actually spending time with the baby. She had the child brought to her in the mornings after she'd been fed and clothed and was usually in a happy, sunny sort of mood.

If all babies were as delightful as this one, Lionel found himself thinking with no small amount of surprise, he might be predisposed to go ahead and have one before the five years he'd imagined he would wait were up.

"Is she always like this?" he asked on one such morning. They had finished their breakfast and the staff of nannies had brought Jules in. Geraldine didn't seem to care that her cadre of stylists dressed her exquisitely every morning for his pleasure, not hers, and he knew this because she had no qualms whatsoever throwing herself down on the floor with the child.

She looked up at him now, her lips curving. "She gets tired and cranky like anyone else, but she really is happy little girl. Just like her mother was."

Sometimes she spoke of her cousin lightly, but other times it was like this. With that weight.

"I never met her when she was happy," he found himself saying, though he could not have said why. "I only knew her when she was impaired."

"You must have met a great many women in various states of disrepair," Geraldine said, perhaps too carefully. Lionel eyed her, though she was concentrating on the baby. "I'm surprised you remember Seanna at all."

"She made an impression."

Her gaze was darker than usual, then. "As you did too, for her. She said your name when she came home. She said it a lot. That's the reason I assumed you were Jules's father."

Lionel set his paper aside and considered Geraldine instead, not at all sure she wanted to head down this road. And there must have been something on his face, because her expression changed.

"I'm not going to faint if you tell me something unpleasant about my cousin," she said quietly. "I was with her through far worse things than I think you can possibly imagine."

A birth, Lionel thought. And a death. And everything that had happened in between.

He could not recall a time he had ever wanted to reach back through time and change things, and not for himself, but so Geraldine did not have to carry that particularly shade of darkness in her gaze just then.

The notion disturbed him, for reasons he did not care to examine. "I met your cousin at the end of a shoot." He spoke quietly, but directly. He did not look away. "The pictures were good but she was a mess. The way others in the room spoke of her was not kind, but they are used to bright stars who rise quickly, then crash and burn. It is not a kind business."

Her eyes were overbright. "You don't have to preface it. You can just tell me."

"She knew who I was and she made overtures," Lionel said, still not moving his gaze from hers. "I declined."

"And what about you?" Geraldine's voice was so quiet then, so rough, he barely heard it over the baby's pleased little gurgles. "Were you cruel to her, too?"

"I was not." He watched as she looked down, then swallowed hard enough that he could see her throat move. "I told her that she deserved better, but that she would never find it if she did not first value herself."

Geraldine was looking at Jules, her expression fierce enough that Lionel suspected she was trying to keep her tears at bay. "I am not sure she took your advice."

"She had what I would describe as a moment of lucidity." Lionel remembered the way the girl had looked at him, her dull eyes too big in her face, her body far too thin. "And she told me that her value was set by the marketplace, and didn't I know? That was what it meant to be a commodity."

Geraldine flinched, but no tears marked her cheeks.

"And so I told her that she had mistaken the matter entirely," Lionel said, not gently. That would have seemed too easy. It would not have done the lost Seanna any justice—though he could not have explained why he felt such a thing. "That her value was inherent. That all she needed to do was believe it and she would find it."

He blew out a breath, not sure why a chance encounter some time ago got to him like this one did. It was tempting to think it was because he knew that she was Geraldine's cousin, but he hadn't known Geraldine existed back then and still, he remembered. He remembered the bruised look around the girl's eyes. The way she'd laughed after he'd said those things to her, and how that spark had changed her entirely. He had seen a glimpse of who she might have been, there for a moment, then gone.

I don't think that's where I'm going, she'd told him, with a wisdom—a knowledge—he had found chilling.

Lionel remembered asking after her, months

later, and being told she had disappeared the way so many did.

These girls are disposable and replaceable, he had been told, dismissively. *Better not to ask what they get up to once they go, no?*

He did not share those things with Geraldine. And not only because he knew exactly how Seanna's story had ended. That she had been right about her trajectory.

"I think," Geraldine said, her voice sounding as if this was far more difficult for her than she wished him to know, "that you must have stood out. It's my impression that she did not otherwise encounter much kindness."

"The world is not usually kind, no," Lionel agreed. "We must find it ourselves, I think."

Geraldine twisted around to face him and there was something darker in her gaze, then. It seemed to punch into him. "That sounds a little too close to placing blame, doesn't it? We can talk about choices. Psychology. Mental health. Parenting." She handed the baby the toy she had just tossed aside with her usual infant glee. "But in the end, do any of us know why one life goes one way and another a different way?"

"Indeed we do," he replied darkly, as much because he felt as if she'd punched him as anything else. "Lives are like anything else. They're made up of choices. And ego. Do you make your choice for yourself or for something greater than yourself? I was raised by two generations of men who thought of nothing but their own pleasure. Ever. I do not make the same choices they did. On purpose."

"I don't think Seanna was overly concerned with pleasure." Geraldine took a heavy sort of breath. "I think she was trying to hide." Then she looked at him again, and her gaze was clear. He didn't think that made things any better. "But is that why you are so determined to do as your grandmother asks? To make up for your father and grandfather?"

"If I could make up for them, I would." Lionel didn't know why he was having this conversation, when it had seemed to slip so far beyond his control. Or why he could *feel* too many things jostling about inside of him. When he did not indulge *feelings*.

Just as he did not talk about lost girls he had failed to save or the bitter inheritance the men in his family had left him.

What was it about this woman that made him unlike himself? Why couldn't he view her with the same calm and distant regard he did everything else?

"I don't think any of us can make up for another person," Geraldine said softly, her gaze a little too intense for a moment before she shifted it once again to the child. "All we can do is be the best version of ourselves."

And he was not sorry that he had to take a call then, though he assured himself it was in no way a *relief.* Because he was Lionel Asensio and he did not look for ways to avoid uncomfortable conversations. He reveled in them.

Or he always had before.

Possibly because you have never had anything at stake, a voice inside him suggested.

He did not believe he had anything at stake now, he assured himself. And was perhaps even more inflexible in a negotiation than usual later that day, to prove it. Because he had nothing to prove. Because he felt nothing.

Because he had decided a long, long time ago that feelings were for the weak.

Yet soon enough, weak or not, the sun went down and he could once again sit across from Geraldine at their little table in the garden.

Lionel had never taken his meals out in this garden before her. He had lived in this house for years, preferring his own space to what privacy he could cobble together at the main house. But he had always viewed this as a place of duty. He was far happier moving between his various offices around the world than staying here too long, mired in memories of his childhood.

He could not recall the last time he'd spent so many consecutive days on the estate. And yet with Geraldine here, he found he did not think back to a great many of those memories as he'd always assumed he would. Lionel was far more concerned with her.

Because during the day she could ignore him. She

could pretend she didn't understand the references he made to the way this honeymoon should have been progressing, if it was traditional.

Everything was different at night.

It was because of the food, perhaps, because Andalusian cuisine never failed to impress and his cook was a wonder. Perhaps it was the wine, sourced from the Asensio vineyards, and always the perfect accompaniment.

Perhaps it was these sultry fall nights themselves. Because in the depths of all the shadows, as the nights grew cooler, Lionel found he could see far different truths than were visible in the light of day.

Tonight there was something edgier than usual, there in the flickering candlelight between them.

Tonight everything seemed…a little bit brighter. A little bit hotter.

They had taken their time over the meal and were sitting there now it was done, speaking of everything and nothing. Lionel wasn't certain when this had become their habit.

He wasn't sure he had ever had *habits* where women were concerned. Not ones that involved anything outside the bedroom.

And if he was tempted to *feel* something about this strange turn of events, he reminded himself that he had never had a wife before, either.

He did not *feel* anything, he told himself. He simply wanted her, and so he stood—enjoying a little too much the way her eyes widened. The way whatever she had been telling him about the Spanish language course she had started taking on her mobile simply…stopped. Midsentence.

"Dance with me," he commanded her.

Or perhaps he was kidding himself. Perhaps it was an invitation, no command, just entreaty.

And he waited, when he had never waited. When he was so tired of waiting. When *waiting* was beginning to sit in his bones, making them ache.

Lionel's whole body tightened with that same bright fire, that same wild need that these days had only honed to an ever-sharpening hunger.

Geraldine gazed up at him from the table, her fine lips parting as if she could taste it too, this maddening *thirst*.

"Don't be silly," she said, but she hardly sounded like herself. Her voice was low and rough. "There is no music."

"There is always music, *mi media naranja*," he murmured. "If you listen hard enough, you will hear it."

Then he held out his hand.

And he did not pretend that he could not feel the heat between them, now. Or that this was precisely the sort of inflection point they had been talking about earlier.

A moment to choose.

Lives were choices, he had told her earlier with such great confidence.

Lionel could not pretend to be unaware that this was one. Right here. Right now.

And more, that he had already made his choice. That what remained was hers, whatever that might be.

He might have been known as a titan in the boardroom, but he always knew the answer to any question he asked where his business was concerned. He could not say the same about Geraldine.

Her eyes were whole worlds he had not explored, though he wanted to.

God, how he wanted to.

But it was as if the barriers between them, all the resistance that she had been attempting to put up for weeks, simply *shimmered* tonight. As if all the barriers between them were a bit thinner than usual.

She looked at his hand for too long, and then, very slowly, Geraldine lifted her fathomless green gaze to his face.

And something inside of him jolted, electric and intense.

Because Lionel knew. He knew, at last, that she would be his.

Finally, something in him roared, as much in triumph as heat.

Geraldine shifted in her chair. Then she reached out and slid her hand into his, and they both let out a sound at that.

As if neither of them could help it.

His was deeper, more of a growl. Hers sounded to him like some kind of gasp.

He wanted to taste it. He wanted to taste her, everywhere.

But first there was this. The touch of her skin to his. Her palm in his hand. The heat of her, that satin smoothness that already haunted him. That was deep in him, making his hunger near enough to overwhelming.

Lionel pulled her to him, or she stood and moved herself—but either way, she was in his arms.

At last, *at last*, she was in his arms again.

And he remembered, distantly, dancing with her at his grandmother's celebration. It seemed a lifetime ago now. It seemed to him that they had been different people entirely, strangers, nothing like who they were now.

Yet even then, he had felt this driving hunger for her. That he had wanted to clear the whole ballroom. Looking back, all he could recall was the two of them, spinning around and around, shining with all of this need and wonder.

He had felt too many things to name.

He had *felt*.

Because it was a mad burst of impossible light, filling both of them at once with the same fire, as if it had always been meant for them. Dancing had made it worse. Dancing had made it *obvious*.

That there was this thing between them, far more than mere heat. Far more complicated than anything that could be sorted out in a bed—

But Lionel didn't like that thought at all.

So instead of teaching her to dance to the music of the moon alone, and feeling whatever questionable emotions that might bring, he bent his head and took her mouth with his.

CHAPTER NINE

THIS KISS WAS nothing like the last one.

That was the last full thought Geraldine had, as Lionel's stern mouth opened over hers and he licked his way between her lips.

And then her whole life seemed to burst into flame.

As if there was *before* this moment and *after* this moment—this impossible kiss—but she was not the same. And never would be the same, ever again.

She had the idle notion that she should care about that, but it disappeared at the taste of him. That stunning hit that was part wine, part smoke, and all him.

Because she'd had no idea.

No earthly idea that it was possible that anything could ever taste like he did, or that she had been walking around all this time, all her life, having no idea that *this* was something people could just *do*.

That she could have been doing since the moment she'd met him.

He kissed her and he kissed her, angling his jaw,

and pulling her body even closer to his, so that she was *pressed* up against him.

Geraldine had never known such heat. She had never understood the spinning, lustrous, silken darkness of this, and the sheer glory of it, too.

He kissed her and introduced her to herself.

A version of her Geraldine had never known.

She learned that a kiss was not a finite thing. That it grew and changed, shifting as they did, taste and heat and fire. She learned that the ache in her breasts was to encourage her to press herself against the wide planes of his chest, the soft parts of her against the hard heat of him.

It was the only thing that made her feel better and then, immediately, she only wanted more.

More and then still more. More and more and *more*.

She understood her body in a new way, now, because all the different parts of her were filled with that same aching electricity, and seemed to match his.

Exactly.

Geraldine could even feel his arousal against her belly, and though she'd read about such things in too many books to count, she had never understood that it could *feel* like this.

As if the entire course of human history had led unerringly to this moment. To the two of them in this garden. To the things she learned about herself when she could melt into him and press herself against him, seeking that knife-edge relief that became longing almost in the same moment.

That she could want nothing more than to take him into her body, or rub herself against him, or do what she actually did—twine her arms around his neck as if she knew that was what he wanted most, then let him lift her straight off the ground.

She had known this would happen, hadn't she? She had decided to stay. She had stood out in the dark, looking at him through the glass, and she had known.

That that decision to remain here meant that she was choosing this. That she had decided to allow this to happen.

That really, this was what she'd wanted all along.

But then she hadn't quite understood how a person went from *decisions* to *actions*, not in a case like this. All the research in the world, all the books and articles, couldn't help her read a stern, beautiful man. Much less tell her when and how he might decide to *do something* about that gleaming thing she had seen in his gaze all along.

So she had waited. And she had meant it when she'd told him that she understood the function of a honeymoon period, even if it didn't involve the act most honeymoons were dominated by. She'd told herself, nightly, that she was enjoying the opportunity to get to know Lionel in a way she doubted anyone else did, not even his fearsome grandmother.

Then again, perhaps she'd known all along that it would take one touch.

One simple touch, and they would ignite.

And with that same deep wisdom, welling up from somewhere she couldn't access deep inside herself, Geraldine knew something else, too. There would be no returning from this. There would be no going back.

Maybe she had always suspected that would be true. Maybe she had wanted to hold on to what she knew, the odd domesticity that she and Lionel had created here over the course of the last few weeks.

Maybe she had been mourning the loss of what felt very much like an ease between them, as unlikely as that should have been.

But what she understood now was that there wasn't a single part of her that wanted to go back. To undo this. To keep her hands to herself and take herself to her own bed, alone again.

Because she might not know what this night would bring, but she wanted every part of it. With every single thing that made her who she was, with every touch of his lips to hers, and every breath that made her breasts move against him yet again.

She wanted *everything*.

When Lionel lifted his mouth from hers, he was carrying her into that great room of his but he was not stopping in the great, glassed-in space. He strode through it, carrying her into a bedroom that was built on the same grand scale. Only this one was not made of glass. There were windows on one side and a vast bed that made her stomach feel funny inside her, but he carried her instead to the seating area arranged before an imposing fireplace, then laid her carefully upon the soft and cozy sheepskin rug that stretched before the dancing flames.

And better yet, followed her down.

"I feel as if I have waited for this for whole lifetimes," Lionel growled in her ear.

Geraldine felt the goose bumps prickling into life up and down her arms, but then he was pressing her back into the soft embrace of the sheepskin beneath her. And he was holding her face in his hands, kissing her and kissing her, then muttering things in that dark, evocative way of his—Spanish and English and other languages like lines of poetry that all wound around her and then deep into her.

He peeled back the bodice of her dress and found her breasts with his hands, making low, approving noises at their weight, their shape. Then he continued on, taking the dress with him, until he moved the faintly rough surface of his palms over just about every part of her that she could imagine and tossed the dress aside when he was done.

Lionel sat back, taking a moment to look down at her with an expression on his face that she'd never seen before.

It made her heart hurt as it beat too hard inside her. Because he looked possessive. Intent.

Mine, she thought, though she knew better than to say such a thing out loud.

Or even think it so he might suspect it lived inside her.

And the harsh lines of his face seemed somehow more sensual now, even though she supposed he should have looked something like scary, gripped as he was in that same heat that shook through her again and again.

Making her feel a delightful kind of feverish.

Geraldine sat up because she needed her hands on him, too, in a way that felt like an actual, physical necessity rather than some kind of longing.

She moved on her knees to kneel beside him and she thought she would die if she didn't tip forward and put her mouth to his neck. So she did and it was overwhelming and seductive and the taste of his skin moved in her like its own mad heat, making her fumble with the buttons of his shirt.

Not because she didn't know how to unbutton something, for God's sake, but because she never had from this angle. Not when the buttons that she was undoing were on the shirt of a man.

And not just any man, but this one.

This man. Lionel Asensio, who had been living in her head for much too long.

Geraldine had considered hers a *life of the mind* for a long, long while, but she already knew that she could never go back to it. Not now that she knew the sheer, sultry perfection of the line of a man's neck and where it met his shoulder. The rough-sweet taste. The scent of him, bold and all-consuming.

She pushed the shirt from his shoulders and made a little sound in the back of her throat because he was more beautiful than she could possibly have imagined, and she had done some extensive imagining lately. She let her fingers move over the dusting of hair she found before her until they dragged over his nipples, and she thought that it was an unbearable marvel that they should both have them. That they could match here, too. That touching him there made her own nipples tighten and point toward him, as if they knew things she didn't.

She trailed her fingers down his ridged wonder of an abdomen, and it was the same kind of wonder. Everywhere she touched him made that corresponding part of her...*bloom.*

And no one had told her. No one had explained that this was the reason why people went mad for each other in ways she had never understood. Why sex was an obsession. Why the most astonishing decisions seemed to be made in pursuit of it.

Because Geraldine already knew that she would do anything to do this again. She could already tell that this was not enough. That it was possible—that it was *likely*—that nothing ever would be.

She took her time exploring him, aware that she could feel the lick of the flames as if they were leaping from the grate—but no. It was the fire they made between them. The tinder of her mouth against his skin, her fingers learning every inch of him.

But when she got down to the waist of his trousers, he stopped her.

"One night," he told her and his voice was deliciously rough, its own kind of caress as it moved over her, "I will tutor you in what, precisely, brings me pleasure. But that will not be tonight, *mi media naranja*. Tonight we have other things to consider."

"Like what?" Geraldine asked, her voice hoarse. Because she could see the outline of his sex, huge and hard, changing the shape of him as she looked down.

Between her legs, she felt herself grow slick and hot.

Ready, something in her pronounced.

"You are an innocent," he said. "A virgin. This is not so?"

His voice changed as he said that, so she sat up straighter. He had gone stern. His dark eyes glittered. And there was something about the way he looked at her, as if sizing her up, that made her shiver to attention. "I am."

"Why did you attempt to lie about this before?"

"Why did you think it was appropriate to ask?" she countered, but her voice was a bare scratch of sound.

She was breathing too heavily, she realized. As if she was running somewhere when all she was doing was kneeling before him, her breasts caught up in that lacy bra they'd put her in tonight. And still wearing the lacy panties they'd given her, too.

Geraldine did not have to ask him to understand that he knew, to the last millimeter of fabric, exactly what she wore. And exactly how the flush of desire, heat and hope, rolled over her.

He knew everything here, she understood.

And she liked that he did. It made her feel safe. Protected.

As if she might survive this fire between them after all.

"This is how it will be," he told her, very sternly, his words like cool stones against her heated flesh. "I want you pink and breathless. I'm going to make you come, Geraldine. Again and again. Until you beg me for things you cannot even imagine."

"I've done a great deal of studying—" she began.

But he reached over and traced her lips with his thumb, silencing her that easily.

"You will not speak again," he told her in that same deliberately stern way. "Unless you wish to say my name. You may cry it out. You may sob it. You may let it fall out in a sigh. But that is all I will allow. There will be no questions. There will be no unsolicited dissertations. Do you understand me?"

And she wondered if, at another time, she might question how she felt in this moment. But right now, Geraldine found she did understand.

More than that, she thought that the rules made everything feel easier.

"You will not focus on anything except what you feel," he told her in that same formidable way. And while he spoke he moved closer, so he could trace a lazy sort of pattern in that hollow between her breasts. "If I want you to do something, I will tell you not only what I wish you to do, but how to do it. You do not have to worry about anything except following my instructions. Do you understand?"

But even as she began to form a response, she saw that dark brow lift. Only his name, he had told her. And only in the ways he had laid out.

Geraldine swallowed hard. She had never taken direction like this in her life. She was not one for taking direction at all, if she was honest about it.

Yet nothing in all her years had ever felt as right as the way she held his gaze with hers and nodded. *Yes. I understand.*

Her reward was the curve of his hard mouth. *"Buena chica."*

Then he set himself to his work.

And Geraldine knew that she had no frame of reference here. No one had touched her like this. No one but her had ever looked at the whole of her body. No one had ever stripped her naked as he did, then laid her out before him.

No one had ever touched her the way he did then, taking his time. Making her flush and buck and moan.

She knew she didn't have the experience to put this into context, but she couldn't imagine that there was any other way this could have happened that would have allowed her to feel so...*free*.

Geraldine didn't think. She didn't question him.

He told her what to do and she did it.

"Turn over," he said at one point, his voice sheer gravel.

And that was its own sort of wonder, as she'd pressed herself into the fluffy embrace of the rug below her with the heat of him at her back. His mouth and his hands finding new ways to make her sing.

The way she could feel that rampantly male part of him as he entertained himself, preview and promise all at once. The way other times he simply moved about, tasting her here, touching her there.

He flipped her over again and this time, explored her body as if it was entirely new because he was using his mouth.

Lazily, he made his way down the length of her torso. He took his time with each one of her breasts, introducing her to erogenous zones she hadn't known she possessed, like her navel. Like the soft skin behind her knees.

Only when she was shaking already did he settle himself between her legs.

"Lionel..." she managed to get out.

And when he looked up at her, there was a glint in those dark eyes—something like approval—and she felt that quake through her.

All that before he pulled her legs up higher, so

that he was holding her thighs apart and letting her legs dangle down over his shoulders.

Geraldine didn't know if she was shocked or horrified, delighted or simply mad with need. All of the above, perhaps.

She was shaking and shaking. She was too *hot*.

Her hips were lifting of their own accord. Her eyes drifting shut. And she couldn't bear the intensity of this. She couldn't bear to look at him as he moved over her in this way, or as his fingers found their way into the core of her, into all her sleek and secret heat, and began to play her like some kind of instrument.

He made her into a melody she had never heard in her life, not like this, and it made her feel as if she was dancing.

It made her throw back her head and sing the only song she could.

His name.

Again and again, his name.

And that was how she found her first peak, then hurtled over it, still singing out that same song.

But she had no time to gather herself because he kept going, shifting even lower, so he could begin to lick his way all over the molten center of her need, teaching her things she could never have known otherwise.

How to melt and bloom into his mouth. How to grip his thick hair in fists.

How to ride him as he ate at her, as if her hips held a wisdom of experience she could only guess at.

And all the while, the need in her only grew.

This time, when she exploded, she screamed.

He took his time as she floated down from that, shifting their positions. Laying himself out beside her and kissing her again, so she could taste her own mysteries on his mouth while she could feel his hugeness, hard and rampant against her belly.

Lionel took her to the peak and beyond once more, this time plunging one finger and then another deep inside her, stretching her, readying her—

God, she thought, *I am so ready—*

And it was as if he could read her very thoughts. For only then did he move between her legs and settle himself there, the heavy weight of him pressing her down into the soft rug and the hard floor beneath it.

He reached down between them so he could take the thick head of his sex and begin to make his way inside her at last.

"Geraldine," he warned her when she moaned. "I have told you the rules."

That made her shudder all over again, but she whispered his name.

Then moaned it as he began working himself inside her.

It wasn't that it didn't hurt, because it did. But her sob was his name and every time she cried out it felt like a connection and her body surrendered just that little bit more.

Then just a little bit more than that.

And soon enough, she could feel him crowding

inside of her, the very tip of him flush against a part of her that she had never felt before.

Geraldine was panting. She felt as if she couldn't pull in a full breath.

But he had told her that she had only one word at her disposal and it worked that same magic every time she used it.

So she cried out his name until she needed to move her hips, and that was how the first wave of impossible pleasure crashed into her. So wild and so intense, so *everything*, that she couldn't quite tell if she was arching her back because she wanted it to go on forever or if it was simply the most intense pleasure she had ever felt.

So she did it again.

And then again.

She kept doing it until Lionel laughed, gathering her against him and dropping his face to the side of her neck. Then he began to teach her all over again.

The thrust, the retreat. The friction. The heat.

And the peaks she'd reached before were hills, she saw that now. This was too big, too intense, to bear.

Geraldine wondered if she should have been afraid, but she wasn't.

There was nothing she wanted more than *this*. Than him.

She arched against him, meeting each thrust. She wrapped her legs around him, dug her nails into his back, and she used his name again and again. A song, a whisper. A moan, a sob.

Because it was bigger every time. It was everything. There was nothing in the world but the enormity of this thing that rushed for her then.

And the pace he'd maintained, ruthless and inexorable, broke. Lionel made a noise, animal and wild, and it took her a moment to understand that he was saying her name this time.

Then there was no rhythm at all.

There was only him inside her, there was only the endless sensation, and her certain knowledge that she would do anything at all to keep going. That nothing could possibly stop them.

That nothing would be worth stopping for—

She felt that mountain slam into her, then throw her—spinning and shimmering—straight out into space.

Until she became the stars.

She could feel the way he said her name edge itself into her, changing her, marking her forever.

She could feel the way he gripped her even tighter, and then scalded her so that her own wild pleasure started all over again.

Geraldine would never be the same. She had known that going in.

But she also knew, as he dropped his head to hers, that she was forever altered. That her heart beat with his and always would, now. That she had fallen recklessly and dreadfully in love, and there was no changing it.

More than that, she knew that she could never tell him. No matter what.

So she told him the only thing she could. Geraldine turned her face to his and though she felt the moisture on her face, she pressed the faintest kiss to his temple anyway. She whispered his name.

Again and again, until Lionel lifted his head, fixed her with a look she recognized now, and started all over again.

CHAPTER TEN

LIONEL HAD WANTED HER. He had intended to have her, and so he had.

Over and over again.

What he had not expected was that having her would become an obsession. That she was a kind of need that only deepened and sharpened as time went by.

That *she* was far more than he had anticipated, in every possible way.

He told himself it was because he'd waited, that was all. It was because of how unfamiliar it had been to find himself wanting something he hadn't been able to sample at once. Perhaps it was no more than a message, letting him know that he had become far too spoiled by his wealth and the privilege it accorded him to have his every need met instantly.

That was why weeks passed and he was still consumed with her, he assured himself. He was making up for that unexpected deficit.

With no end in sight.

The honeymoon period his grandmother had set for them ended, but nothing changed between them. Lionel found his interest in Geraldine intensified, if anything, which hardly made sense. Familiarity bred contempt. Everyone knew this. It had always been his experience before—but Geraldine was different.

In every possible way, she was different.

For example, Lionel had never brought his women here to the estate, and some had begged him for the chance. But he had always refused, because he had never allowed the women he'd had relationships with access to his life like this.

Not to his childhood home. Not to the land that his family had held for so many generations. And never, ever into his grandmother's orbit.

When he had conceived of marrying to please his *abuelita*, he had imagined that after the birthday party, the wife he'd chosen would take herself off to one of his properties elsewhere. He hadn't minded which one. He had expected he would need to trot out the wife on special occasions, and would otherwise plead his busy life.

His grandmother would have seen through him, but that hadn't worried him. Doña Eugenia knew better than most why her grandson was the way he was. Lionel had been sure that when she saw how easily he planned to get along with the wife he bought—and he'd planned it that way, so he knew it would have been that way—she would come around.

He had not been prepared for the Cartwright heiress to be stolen out from under him or for Geraldine to laugh her way to the altar.

But then, Lionel also would have said that he had no interest in spending time with an infant. He'd never been all that interested in having babies, even though he was well aware that he was required to procreate to keep the fortune in the family.

That had always seemed to be a problem he could deal with far off in the future, if at all.

Now Geraldine was his wife. She lived in his house. She slept in his bed. And she would have spent every minute of every day with little Jules if she could, which meant he spent time with her too.

And somehow none of his rules seemed to apply to either one of them.

"Have you spoken to your mother?" Lionel found himself asking one evening, which was in and of itself astonishing.

He assumed that all the women he'd been involved with before had also been in possession of mothers, but he had never inquired. It had never occurred to him to wonder about people so wholly distant and unconnected to him. Yet here he was, the very picture of domesticity all of a sudden.

He was sitting in that great room of his, before the fire. He was gazing about warmly as if it had always been his dearest wish to spend his evenings with a woman he had already explored thoroughly and a happy baby that was not his own.

What he should have been, he kept telling himself,

was outraged, for Geraldine had clearly cast some kind of spell on him.

But he could never quite work himself up into any kind of outrage, no matter how he tried. And if Geraldine thought the question about her mother was strange, she kept it to herself. "I speak to my mother all the time. At least three times a week."

That surprised him. Maybe that was the reason Geraldine was so firmly lodged beneath his skin—he never knew what she was going to say or do. She had never bored him yet.

"Even after she left here the way she did?" he asked.

Geraldine was sitting on the rug the way she liked to do, supervising Jules as she gurgled with delight and flung the toy she was holding as far as she could. Over and over again. Every time, with a patience that Lionel could only admire, Geraldine would pick up the toy, smile at the little girl, and hand it back to her.

And when he asked her that question, Geraldine laughed. "My mother and I have always had a peculiar relationship. It's almost as if neither one of us can bear how much we care for the other. We do better when we are simply discussing our lives with each other, not looking for support, just sharing the details. It's when there are expectations of particular emotional responses that we are less successful. But my aunt and my cousin never really got along at all, so believe me, I can tell the difference."

She smiled down at the baby with such joy that it

made something in Lionel seem too tight. He found himself pressing the heel of his palm to his chest to dissipate it.

But Geraldine was still talking. "I think my aunt was always afraid of Seanna's beauty and what it would mean. And I suppose you could say she wasn't wrong, given how it ended up. She ended up blaming Seanna, as if she'd meant to be that beautiful and therefore meant everything else to happen too."

"My mother took it as a personal affront that she was ever expected to pay any attention to me," Lionel told her, and shrugged when she looked at him, her eyes wide. "She had already suffered through the pregnancy. And the indignity of a lifelong scar on her abdomen, forever ruining her figure."

"Lionel…"

"In truth, I was always grateful that she did not pretend otherwise. It was easier."

He meant that, but the words hung there in the room, seeming heavy next to the way Jules laughed and clapped. And Geraldine looked for a moment as if she might cry.

And this, Lionel told himself, was yet another reason he avoided feelings at all costs. He preferred that he always knew precisely what went on in the rooms he inhabited. That there were clear agendas to follow and obvious signs indicating what was happening and to whom.

Allow emotion in and there were undercurrents and uncertainties. There were *kind eyes* and overbright glances and too much he did not want to think about, like the mother who had excluded herself from consideration years ago.

"Some say she deliberately infected herself with the bacterial infection that killed her," Lionel found himself saying. "I doubt that, but she certainly did nothing to protect herself against it when she could have. It's not as if it was an easy thing to catch. What I do know is that all she cared about once she was ill was the planning of her funeral. She wanted to make sure that it was a grander function than any party my father might throw to celebrate himself, in life or death. That was their primary relationship, you understand. Base competition."

"Surely not." But she wasn't arguing, Lionel saw. She only *wanted* what he was saying not be true.

"She could have gotten treatment," Lionel said, and he didn't know why reciting these facts made his ribs ache. "She knew she was ill. She might even have suspected what it was. Instead, she died within the week, though she did make certain to tell me that she was delighted she wouldn't have to pretend to care about any children I might have one day."

That sat even more heavily in the middle of the room, filling it up until he was surprised that the glass ceilings didn't crack and rain shards down upon them.

"My mother and I get along marvelously, really," Geraldine said softly, and the wideness in her eyes turned to a kindness that he did not wish to see. Or feel behind his ribs. "But she didn't want me to take care of Seanna either, if for different reasons. Everyone else in the family thought we should let Jules get adopted and pretend Seanna had just…gone off somewhere. My mother didn't think that, necessarily, but she was concerned at what nursing Seanna would do to me. Personally. And what taking on a child on my own might do to me, also personally. It's a critical distinction, you see."

Lionel did not see.

As if she could tell, Geraldine smiled, and that made that pressure in his chest worse. "I mean that she worries about me, not what people might say about her or our family. That's why she left. It might look like judgment, but it's not. It's that she can't bear to stay and watch me do things she worries might hurt me." It was her turn to shrug. "Love doesn't have to look the way you think it should, Lionel."

Later that night, when she came back from putting the baby to sleep and joined him for their usual dinner, he stripped her of the clothes she wore and laid her out on that very same rug, where the glass hadn't shattered and the room still felt too full.

And he did everything he could to make her scream.

Though he refused to ask himself what he thought he was proving. Or what he thought he meant by it.

Lionel kept waiting for the spell to be broken as the days passed. Fall rolled in, limning the fields with a deeper gold. The sky was a far more intense blue overhead. And the green of Geraldine's eyes seemed to grow more mysterious.

If anything, he felt more enchanted by her, not less.

Yet having taken that month that his grandmother had ordered, though he had worked despite her demands, he had to go back to his usual travels. And at first, he assumed that he would enjoy his visits to different offices around the globe the way he always had. The excitement of waking up in a new city. The challenge of walking into a different office.

But he did not find it all as thrilling as he had before.

Historically, no matter how much he enjoyed a relationship, Lionel had always been grateful for his work. Because he enjoyed that as well—and often far more, if he was honest. When he was in the office, he had always been perfectly capable of compartmentalizing. Not that he would have called it that.

He simply didn't think about the woman in his life until and unless he wanted to see her.

But he thought about Geraldine all the time.

In the middle of the tense negotiation in a boardroom in Singapore one evening, he found his mind wandering as he wondered what Geraldine was going to do with her morning with him away. And whether she missed him when he traveled—

When Lionel realized the direction of his thoughts, he sat back in his chair, so shocked he had to cough to cover the growl of dismay he was sure he'd made audibly.

For never, in all of his life, could he recall ever wondering—for even a moment—if anyone missed him.

He was Lionel Asensio.

On some level, he supposed, he had always rather thought that the lights dimmed when he quit a room.

When he came back from that trip, he found Geraldine fast asleep in the bed they now shared. Because he had insisted that she move into his rooms. *For the access,* he had assured himself. *For the convenience,* he had told her.

Tonight he stood there watching the moonlight play over her, for far too long. Fully clothed.

For far longer than he would have admitted if she'd woken up to see him at it.

Eventually, he talked himself out of whatever daze he was in. He'd showered off the mess in his head, then slipped into the bed beside her, waking her up in the best way he could imagine.

Every time he came home, it was the same. Whether she was asleep or awake, she always greeted him with the same obvious delight. The same sweetness, the same fire.

And every time he tasted her anew, he was certain that this would be the time that it failed to excite him as it had before. That she would fall short of the memories he tortured himself with when he was away.

It was possible he looked forward to that happening, but it never did.

Instead, every time, it was better.

Because he had taught her everything she knew and she was a clever student. He could do nothing but exult in the way she set about attempting to master each and every skill he'd introduced her to.

Until some nights, it was hard to remember who had taught who.

"I need something to do," she told him one day, when they had been together some while. They were walking outside along the fields, taking in the cooler air. "I'm not used to all this inactivity."

"You are an Asensio wife," he intoned, as if that was all that should matter to her.

There was a primitive part of him that thought it was, in fact, the only thing that should matter to her. But there was also a part of him that liked her more than he wanted to for saying such a thing, because *he* certainly wouldn't have liked sitting around, waiting to be dressed and living for her return.

The very idea was absurd.

And Geraldine clearly agreed, as she only rolled her eyes at him.

Lionel felt his mouth curve. "Many women in your position throw themselves into charity work. That is always an avenue that you could choose."

"It's not that I'm opposed to charity," she said after considering it a moment, worrying a stick she'd picked up with her fingers. "That seems so removed, doesn't it? I feel certain that if you or anyone else wants to hand out their money, they will. I'm not sure that I could even discuss such impossibly large sums without laughing."

"Not an ideal tactic in fundraising," Lionel agreed.

But later, when they had a dinner with his grandmother in the private dining salon she used only for family, the *ilustrísima* señora waved two bejeweled hands. "I have been looking for someone I can trust to catalog the Asensio collection," she pronounced as if she had called Geraldine here to the estate for this purpose. "I was beginning to think it would never happen in my lifetime."

"You have a collection?" Geraldine asked, a note in her voice that he had never heard before. When he had heard it before, it had been in the voices of certain men when they discussed race cars. And in the voices of some women when they looked at jewelry. "As in, an actual *collection*, not simply an attic full of sentiment?"

"I am not sentimental," the old woman told her with a sniff. "I am disarmingly shrewd. Ask anyone."

"This is true," Lionel said when his grandmother lifted a brow in his direction. "It has been repeatedly confirmed throughout all the halls of Europe."

And so after dinner, Doña Eugenia herself led them to the grand library that claimed an entire wing of the old, rambling house.

"These are merely all the books that are considered readable," his grandmother said, turning in a circle as she looked up at the floor-to-ceiling shelves, all packed tight. Beside her, Geraldine actually quivered with delight. Lionel knew it when he saw it. "We do not have attics, but we do have any number of outbuildings filled with documents, a great many objects of historical interest, and, of course, any number of books. In all kinds of different languages, last I checked."

And Lionel watched as his wife tried her best not to twirl around herself, possibly letting out a squeal or two.

"It's like Christmas," Geraldine told him later. "My second favorite holiday, but the best one as far as gifts are concerned."

She had a look on her lovely face that he had taken as a challenge, then. And he spent several hours showing her that he, too, could give her the kind of joy she had gotten from the very existence of piles of books. That he could provide whatever she craved.

But he was beginning to wonder if he was the one whose cravings were undoing him.

He had been gone for several days on his latest business trip—about which he remembered only that he'd caught the scent of her, coconut and papaya, on a crowded city street on the other side of the planet—when he walked into his house to find that it smelled like a feast.

"There you are," she said brightly when he found her in the semiformal dining room. She clapped her hands together, a lot like Jules did. Then she held them out over the table, which it took him long moments to realize held any number of dishes. "I have been in collusion with the kitchen and they prepared a proper Thanksgiving dinner for us." When he only stared at her, she tilted her head to one side. "You went to school in the States. I know you must have an idea of what Thanksgiving is."

"Of course I do," Lionel said gruffly. But he did not tell her that his memories of that North American holiday were some of his favorites. That he had loved the convivial notion of the holiday that was simply about gathering together and sharing a meal, something he dearly missed when he was not in Spain.

"Thanksgiving is my favorite holiday," Geraldine told him, as if she was sharing a secret.

Lionel sat with her, and the baby, who both laughed too much. That was the trouble. There was all the *smiling.* Even the baby gurgled happily when he looked at her, as if she knew him.

As if you really are her father, something in him suggested.

And he already knew, didn't he, that the notion didn't horrify him as it should have. As he wanted it to.

As he told himself it would have if it weren't for Geraldine, who had gone to the trouble of making it clear she thought about him too much when he was gone. Who indicated, again and again, that she not only listened to the things he told her, she took them into account. She *considered* him.

Over and over again, she made it clear that he mattered to her.

Him. Lionel, the man.

Not the businessman, the billionaire, the heir to the Asensio wealth and power.

He told himself he was tired, that was all, or too full after their American feast, but he knew that it was more than that. Because he was getting too comfortable here. This was all entirely too comfortable. It would be easier if he could convince himself that she had set this whole thing up from the start. That this was all a game she was playing. That she was only pretending...

But he knew better.

He knew innocence when he tasted it. And Geraldine was the worst actress he'd ever encountered. There were some women who could pull off a fake like that, but she wasn't one of them. She never would be one of them.

That was the trouble with her in a nutshell.

Later that night, after she put Jules to bed, Geraldine came and found him. She slipped her arms around him from behind as he stood at the glass windows of his favorite room and looked out into the dark.

Though what he saw was her reflection, superimposed over this land he'd been raised to believe was, truly, the whole of the world.

"Geraldine," he said, because his heart was pounding at him, and he refused to interpret that as anything but a warning. To disengage. To step away from her. To end this, whatever it was. He told himself it could mean nothing else, even if the thought of doing any of those things did not exactly fill him with happiness. *"Mi media naranja..."*

My other half. Why did he keep saying that? Had he made it so?

But she tugged on him so he turned to look down at her. And she smiled up at him, the heat in her gaze so bright that he found he could not resist.

That he did not *want* to resist.

"Tonight," she told him quietly, her green eyes dancing, "you will not speak at all, unless it is my name in your mouth. Do you understand?"

Everything inside him stilled. Then...hummed.

"You play a dangerous game—" he began.

"Lionel," she said, and shook her head as if saddened when still her eyes gleamed with laughter. "That is not my name."

And then, as he stood there, *undone*, she ran her hands down his chest. She took her time. Then her green eyes held his with a kind of solemnity as she knelt down before him.

Then, never looking away from him, she pulled him from his trousers, thick and ready. She wrapped her hands around the base of him, then leaned forward and sucked him in deep.

And she loved him like that, slow and hot, fire and need, undoing him with every low sound she made.

With every stroke of her tongue. With the suction, the heat.

She loved him past the place of no return. She ignored him when he said her name in warning.

And when he finished, despite himself, he shouted out her name.

While inside him, it felt like a song.

She sat back, looking up at him with a smile on her face and what looked like sheer, uncomplicated joy in those green eyes of hers.

And it was as if something in him broke open.

Lionel didn't know what it was. He didn't want to know.

He reached down and pulled her to her feet, then straight into his arms.

And he carried her into the bedroom. Once there, he laid her out on the bed and looked down at her, his heart setting up such a clatter inside his chest that once again, he had to press his own hand to it.

Because it felt as if it might break his ribs.

And for a moment, he could do nothing *but* stand there, his breath coming in too fast. The blood inside him too loud.

For once, he didn't know what he was meant to *do*.

Because Lionel did not feel. He did not *feel things* like this, with an overwhelming need so powerful and so enduring that he was beginning to suspect there was no amount of time spent with her that would ever be enough.

That he would always be caught up in this spell of hers.

But tonight, there was only one word that he could say. And perhaps there was a part of him that was grateful for that, because otherwise he could not trust that he would not say things that he knew he shouldn't.

That he had always vowed he *wouldn't*.

So he crawled up next to her, into her open arms, and then he set about making her his.

All over again.

He pressed his lips to every new swath of skin he uncovered as he removed her clothes. He loved every part of her, and then again.

And he could not tell her what he felt, because he had no vocabulary for such things. And because tonight, there was only her name.

"Geraldine," he whispered, making her name into whole songs.

When she was naked and pink and quivering, he slid his hands beneath her bottom and lifted her up like dessert. Then he sang his favorite song as he licked into her, deep, so it was her turn to scream and lose control completely.

And she was still shuddering when he crawled up the length of her body, still pressing kisses to that sweet, flushed, pink flesh.

He drew her onto his lap so that she knelt astride him, and he waited for her to look down and see where they were joined. Then to pull her lip between her teeth as she looked at him.

And then begin to smile, her eyes shining, as he let her take charge once again.

This time it was a slow, rolling explosion. She rocked against him, wrapping her arms around his neck so she could kiss him as she moved. And there was little he could do but wrap his hands over her hips and enjoy the bright-hot fire between them.

She fanned the flames so they danced higher and higher.

And then, as they both spun out there on the edge, Geraldine pulled her mouth from his and looked down, smoothing her palms over his cheeks to frame his jaw.

Her eyes were darker then. Storm-tossed emeralds, and all his.

"Lionel," she whispered, and his name in her mouth made him thrust harder inside her, deeper and hotter, "I love you."

The words echoed inside him.

I love you.

The words were like a bomb, too huge and too—

But then she bore down, squeezing him tight.

And she sent them both tumbling over the edge, soaring out to all the galaxies they'd made here between them, as if she hadn't ruined everything.

CHAPTER ELEVEN

GERALDINE WOKE UP SLOWLY, found the sun in her face, and her first instinct was to smile.

But in the next moment she realized that if the sun was up, she must have missed Jules's usual morning wake-up routine and so she sat up, frowning, and shoved her hair out of her face.

Only then did she see Lionel sitting in a chair by the fire, staring at her with a dark and brooding sort of look that made him look more like stone than he had in a long while.

It took a moment for the night to come back to her. And then it did, hard, and she knew exactly what this was.

You knew better, she told herself.

"Did you mean it?" he asked, with no preamble.

Geraldine did not pretend she wasn't fully aware what he was asking.

"Te amo," she said, because she'd been practicing. She'd been taking advantage of all the nannies at her disposal and giving herself workdays. She

spent hours in the libraries up at the house, arranging things in preparation for the cataloging that she would only begin in earnest once she learned more Spanish, so she could read everything she found. Lucky for her, Lionel's grandmother was proving to be an excellent and devoted tutor. *"Te quiero. Te quiero con todo mi corazón."*

Because she did love him. With all of her heart.

"I don't understand why you would take this and ruin it in this way," he growled at her.

"What is ruined?" Geraldine asked lightly.

And then watched as Lionel stood and began to pace, which made her heart beat much more rapidly inside her.

Because this was Lionel Asensio. Cool, calm, controlled.

And he seemed to be precisely none of those things just now.

"I cannot have this," he seethed at her, sounding nothing like that stern man of stone she had first met in that Italian chapel. "It was enough that everything was so pleasant. Too pleasant, I grant you. But why couldn't you have left well enough alone?"

"Because I love you."

"You don't."

But Geraldine only smiled.

He made that growling noise again. "You must leave, of course. I have many properties and I'm sure we can find one that will suit you. There's a town house in Manhattan. We can tell my *abuelita* that you wished most fervently to be back in your country."

He scowled when all Geraldine did was shake her head. "I wish no such thing. And she will not believe it anyway. She knows how excited I am to dig into her collection."

"You will stay in Manhattan," he gritted out at her. "Until whatever sickness this is passes."

But something about that made her...almost giddy, she found.

"I'm not sick," she said cheerfully. "In fact, I'm not sure I've ever felt better."

"I should have made this clear." It was almost as if he was talking to himself then, pacing back and forth before the bank of windows with the cold fall morning stretching before him. "It is my fault that I failed to do so."

Geraldine sat up straighter then. She let the covers fall from her, since the fire warmed the room nicely. And then considered herself something close enough to virtuous that she did not smirk at all when his jaw tightened and his dark eyes glittered at the sight of her breasts.

"A long time ago, I had to make a choice," he rasped at her, gravelly and grim. "As we have discussed, my father and his father were wastes of human space. If they were here they would argue with that and say that they simply *followed their feelings* wherever those feelings took them. No matter how dark, how depraved. I made certain that I could never do the same."

"How did you make certain of it?" she asked, careful to keep her voice mild.

Inside, there was that giddiness, but there was something else—and she knew it, now.

It was the way she wanted to be near him, always.

It was the fact that she trusted him, implicitly.

He was the person she most wanted to see when she opened her eyes and the last person she liked to see before she went to sleep. She liked knowing that he was beside her in that enormous bed, wrapped all around her.

She liked his heat. His passion. His intensity in all its forms.

She loved his heart, even though he didn't think he had one.

She loved him.

It was that simple. It was the whole universe. It was her heart, and she was his.

"I am not capable of feeling the kinds of things you want me to feel," he threw at her.

And Geraldine felt too many things at once. A deep sadness for him that he believed this about himself. A kind of wonder that he did not understand that he was already turned inside out, or he would not have thundered at her the way he did.

And beneath all of that, tangled into it, that same wild, wondrous love that had made these weeks glow.

Even if she had wanted to take it back, she wouldn't. She couldn't.

"I don't recall asking you to feel anything for me," she said softly.

And strangely enough, she thought of her cousin. She thought of the ways Seanna had told her again and again that she had tried so hard to love the various men she become entangled with. *I always thought it wouldn't matter if they loved me back,* she had told Geraldine long ago. *That I could love them enough until they did.*

Geraldine could remember thinking that she couldn't understand that kind of math, when it was so clearly never going to add up to anything. And she still believed that.

But she also believed in Lionel.

She believed in all the things he couldn't say, and not because he didn't feel them. She saw the way he looked at her. And not only when they were here, in his bed. She thought of the way he took her hand when they walked. She thought of the way he listened when she spoke, making her the total focus of his world, as if nothing else could ever exist, or ever would.

She thought of how much more often he smiled now. She had even made him laugh a time or two.

And then, wrapped all around these and threaded through it all, was the way he looked at Jules. Geraldine did not have to ask if this man had a great deal of experience with babies. She knew he didn't.

Yet these days it was perfectly natural for him to take Jules in his arms the way he had when he'd come home last night. One morning she'd had to rush out of the room for a moment to get Jules's favorite toy and when she come back, she had found Lionel down on his hands and knees, making the baby squeal with delight.

She had already known that she loved him then.

But it was that morning, that moment, that had made it inevitable that she would tell him so.

That and the way he had looked around at the Thanksgiving feast she'd plotted with the kitchens to prepare for him, then had smiled at her as if she'd personally climbed up into the night sky and fetched him the moon and a sprinkling of stars.

It was the fact that if she could, she would.

"I've spent a lot of time with your grandmother," she told him now, when all he did was glare at her. "She's helping me learn Spanish. But her favorite topic of conversation is you."

"I would strongly urge you not to put too much stock into what my *abuelita* says when it comes to me. She cannot be trusted to tell the truth when she could meddle instead."

"She says it's her fault," Geraldine said quietly, and Lionel looked as if she'd struck him.

There was a part of her that wanted to stop, because she knew that he wouldn't want to have this conversation. But she pushed on.

"That she grew tired of your grandfather and was

disgusted with your father's excesses. She left you here, thinking that there was enough staff about and that you might be all right, because they cared for you better than your own mother did."

She had brought up Lionel's mother with the assumption that he was exaggerating, but had discovered, to her dismay, that he had been underselling it. *That woman was no good,* his grandmother had said quietly.

"Instead, when she returned, you had changed completely. You had been a loving, happy boy, and she'd thought that was simply your personality. That it wouldn't matter what your parents did or didn't do—but she was wrong."

"She has no idea what she's talking about," Lionel said, his voice rising—until he stopped himself. Geraldine thought he might stop talking altogether, but then he shoved his hands through his dark hair. "You don't understand what it was like. Everything was…this feeling or that feeling, as if feelings were facts. As if feelings were more important. As if any promise, or any hope of a promise kept, disappeared in the face of those feelings. It was like walking in quicksand and I decided when I was fourteen that I would do it no longer. There was only one way to find solid ground, and I found it."

He turned toward her then, staring at her with a look on his face that she knew, somehow, he would hate to know he was even capable of making.

But she saw it. And she couldn't stop herself. She

was upon her feet and crossing to him without knowing she meant to move.

And she didn't much care when he looked as if the last thing in the world he wanted was her to touch him. She went to him anyway, sliding her hands up his chest to loop around his neck, and then gazing up at him.

"My grandmother is trying to trick you," he told her stiffly. "She wants the bloodline secured into the next generation."

"I'm sure she does," Geraldine said. But gently. She tipped her head back. "But do you really think she's the sort of woman who cares *only* about bloodlines and family traditions? I've known her for less than a whole season, and I know better. That isn't why she wanted you married. It isn't why she thinks you should have children."

"You cannot possibly think that you know my grandmother better than I do." But his voice was a low scrape of anguish.

Geraldine pressed on. "She loves you. She wants you to know that you are loved. And more, that you *can* love."

But Lionel looked as if he was awash in nothing but misery. "My grandmother is many things, but never has she been mawkish and sentimental."

"She loves you," Geraldine said again. "And let me tell you something about love, Lionel. It's not selfishness dressed up in terms of endearment. It's not self-centered justifications for bad behavior.

You've never told me a single story about your parents that made me think they ever loved anything but themselves. Neither has your grandmother, for that matter. But you aren't anything like them."

And she felt the shudder that went through him then, as if his bones themselves were quaking. She thought he tried to argue, but all that came out was her name.

Like a song he'd once sung, but he'd forgotten the melody.

So Geraldine would remind him. "You love your grandmother beyond reason. You love this land and the legacy of what has been created here, then maintained. You love the people who work for you, here and in all your offices. You treat them like humans, not faceless robots here to do your bidding. You listen with your *whole body*, Lionel. Do you have any idea how rare that is?" She laughed, then, and held him all the tighter. "You are demanding but never imperious, never rude. You simply expect that everyone should be the best version of themselves, including you."

The strong column of his neck worked. "That is simply good business."

"You love Jules," she said softly. "I've seen the way you look at her when you think I'm not paying attention. But I've seen it. And I know."

"Geraldine…" he gritted out.

She slid her palms down so she could press them into his chest. Then she moved one, just slightly, so she could make it clear that she was feeling the way his heart pounded.

And how it pounded even harder once she did it.

Geraldine smiled. "You pride yourself on being cold and unreachable, but you're not. I've seen the way you look at me, too. Every time you look at me."

"I am warning you, Geraldine."

But her smile only widened. "Lionel, I don't know how to break this news to you. And I'm sorry you don't want to hear it. But I'm as certain as I can be that you're in love with me, too."

And it was like watching a hurricane.

The storm wrecked him and she watched it as it happened. She watched it play out in his gaze, in that anguish etched into his face.

She watched it tear him apart.

But then his hands were on her, pulling her closer and spearing his fingers into her hair so he could hold her right there before him.

Not that she wanted to be anywhere else.

"Don't you understand?" he demanded, as if the world was ending. As if, outside, the trees were bent in half beneath the howl of the wind instead of standing prettily beneath a perfectly blue sky. In here, in him, the storm raged. "*What if I do?* That can only mean that I will destroy you, too."

And for a moment the only sound of the storm was the way the two of them breathed, ragged and intense, as if they'd just climbed up something steep. For hours.

"You couldn't destroy me if you tried," she told him when she could speak again. When she could hold her gaze steady on his. When she could make certain he understood that she meant this. "I come from peasant stock, Lionel. I'm built to withstand far greater horrors than the love of a good husband." She leaned in then, sliding her arms around him and holding him close. The way he deserved to be held. "Bring it on, I say."

His arms moved, and she thought for a moment he might try to push her away—*try* being the operative word—but instead he wrapped them around her.

Not exactly gently.

He gazed down at her, stern as stone. "If I love you, Geraldine, there is no going back. There is no escape. There is not only no divorce, there is no separation. I don't like leaving you. Coming home to you is a joy, but I would far rather have you at my side, and I mean that. I mean everything I say and you should know—I am not a man who traffics in half measures. If I say I am in, I will never be out."

"I'm glad to hear it," she shot right back. "Because you do realize, don't you, that you haven't used even a hint of protection with me? That you never even asked?"

And as she watched, then, Lionel Asensio began to laugh.

He laughed, but he held her close until she was laughing, too. And somehow that became kissing, desperate and delighted. Then they were wrapped up in each other, rolling on the bed, and this was as it was supposed to be. This was right.

Geraldine said as much when he worked his way inside her, filling her completely, thrusting in deep. Then deeper still, and yet it was never deep enough.

"You are the only lie I have ever told myself," Lionel growled down at her as he braced himself above her, taking up the whole sky she should have been able to see beyond him. A better view, in her opinion. "Because this is the truth, Geraldine, and it always has been. I want you naked, just like this. I want to be inside you. I want nothing between us, ever. As many children as you wish to give me, I intend to raise. Right here, with you. I want you so much a part of me that it will be as if we are two sides of the same coin. And even that will never be enough."

"Good," Geraldine retorted fiercely. "Because I have been waiting my whole life to love you and I didn't even realize it. It will take me the whole rest of my life to revel in it, and several forevers after that, I would think, for it to sink in."

"Geraldine," he said as he began to move, that slick, hot, perfect rhythm that took everything they were and made it a sweet hot celebration that they could share, over and over again, "I love you. And I promise you, I will love you forever."

So she wrapped herself around him and she fixed her gaze to his. "For richer and for poorer," she told him, because the last vows they'd taken had been a blur, and then she'd fainted.

This felt much better.

"I promise you," he said at once. Then he smiled. "But I must assure you that there is very little possibility that you will ever be anything like poor, *mi media naranja*."

And then, together, they made the only vows that could ever matter.

Here in the chapel of the bed where they found each other, found their way back to each other, and found love wherever they looked.

Over and over again.

CHAPTER TWELVE

LIONEL ADOPTED BABY Jules before her first birthday

"How can she be anything less than mine?" he asked.

"That's how I have felt about her from the start," Geraldine told him, smiling in that way that made her eyes gloss over with emotion.

He would have hated that once, but he was learning.

The presence of an emotion did not mean that the kind of excesses his father was so fond of would follow. It did not mean that, like his grandfather, he would take it upon himself to blow something up— simply because he could.

Geraldine had their second child before Jules was two. A sturdy, green-eyed little boy, who was already so charming, his *abuelita* declared, that surely he would wrap the whole world around his chubby fist before he was five.

In the meantime, Lionel and his beautiful wife made their life together.

They spent time with her family, so that Geraldine's parents could feel easier about the choices she had made. And while they would always be suspicious of his wealth and power—something he grew to appreciate—he thought that over time, they came around.

Then again, that was likely just the grandchildren.

Geraldine learned Spanish at a surprising pace and threw herself into cataloging the Asensio collection, which did not remain a private concern. It was so large and so fascinating that, eventually, they built it a building all its own on the part of the estate that bordered public lands. Then they opened it to anyone who wished to come and view it, and Geraldine got to run the entire operation.

"You have become quite a mogul in your own way," he told her many years later as they arrived for one of the Biblioteca Asensio's grand events that called in scholars and academics, celebrities, and intellectuals from all over the world.

"The thing no one ever tells you," she said, smiling at him with all that laughter in her gorgeous green eyes that she still liked to hide behind her glasses when she was working—because she claimed she couldn't resist the stereotype, "is that moguling is so much *fun*."

"That is a secret," he admonished her, though he was smiling. "You must tell no one, Geraldine. We can't have that kind of thing getting out."

But the real secret, he knew, was love.

They loved each other. They loved their family. They added to it as the years passed. Another boy and then a little girl.

Who they got to watch Jules dote on the way Geraldine had doted on Jules's mother long ago.

They loved each other, and they loved their children, so they never lied to Jules about her parentage. They never kept where she came from a secret, from her or the other children. And they decided that she should be the one to seek out her birth father if she wished. If he could be found.

Though she never showed the slightest inclination to do so.

"All I'd have to say to him is thank you," Jules said when she was older. "He was so terrible, and treated poor Seanna so badly, that he accidentally made my life fantastic. I don't need a single thing from him."

"You," Lionel told her, "are a marvel of a child."

"I take after my mother," Jules told him, laying her head on his shoulder as they watched Geraldine out in the garden, playing with the younger children.

Love was the point of all of it, and that was what Lionel told his grandmother as he sat by her bed as her last days seemed to come much closer than they had before, though she'd made it to the hundredth birthday party she'd vowed she would throw for herself.

She had even made her grandsons dance with her.

"It was a marvelous party, *Abuelita,*" Lionel told her, holding her hand in his.

"I certainly hope so," she responded, with that same old satisfied grin. "Because how else should a life end if not with the celebration? That's the point, *nene.* Love is always the point."

And as the years passed, that was what Lionel remembered.

That life was meant to end, like it or not. And that being so, better that a life should be a celebration of love. Better that it should be marked with joy, and then remembered by those who lived on with laughter, with stories, and with love.

Always and ever love.

If there was a greater legacy than love, Lionel did not wish to know it.

"Aren't you lucky," Geraldine would say when she found him in their bed at night, whether it was at home in Andalusia or in one of their places around the world, where they would stay whenever Lionel needed to travel for work, "that I decided to fall in love with you all those years ago?"

And Lionel knew that he was the luckiest.

But he also knew how to handle his wife. "The lucky one is you, *mi media naranja,*" he would tell her sternly. "And I will have you prove it tonight, I think. By saying only my name. Do you understand?"

She always smiled so wide, his Geraldine.

Then she would whisper his name, as commanded.

But what he heard was *love*, so that was what he gave her. And that was what he got.

And that was what they made, until it was a life, and then it bloomed on into forever.

* * * * *

Were you lost in the passion of
The Spaniard's Last-Minute Wife?
Then don't miss the first installment in
the Innocent Stolen Brides duet
The Desert King's Kidnapped Virgin

And make sure to check out
these other sensational stories
by Caitlin Crews!

Willed to Wed Him
The Christmas He Claimed the Secretary
The Accidental Accardi Heir
A Secret Heir to Secure His Throne
What Her Sicilian Husband Desires

Available now!

#4145 CHRISTMAS BABY WITH HER ULTRA-RICH BOSS
by Michelle Smart

Ice hotel manager Lena Weir's job means the world to her. So succumbing to temptation for one night with her boss, Konstantinos Siopis, was reckless—but oh-so-irresistible. Except their passion left her carrying a most unprofessional consequence... This Christmas, she's expecting the billionaire's heir!

#4146 CONTRACTED AS THE ITALIAN'S BRIDE
by Julia James

Becoming Dante Cavelli's convenient bride is the answer to waitress Connie Weston's financial troubles. For the first time, she can focus on herself, and her resulting confidence captivates Dante, leading to an attraction that may cause them to violate the terms of their on-paper union...

#4147 PREGNANT AND STOLEN BY THE TYCOON
by Maya Blake

Tech genius Genie Merchant will only sell the algorithm she's spent years perfecting to a worthy buyer. When notoriously ruthless Severino Valente makes an offer, their off-the-charts chemistry means she'll entertain it...if he'll give her the baby she wants more than anything!

#4148 TWELVE NIGHTS IN THE PRINCE'S BED
by Clare Connelly

The last thing soon-to-be king Adrastros can afford is a scandal. When photos of his forbidden tryst with Poppy Henderson are sold to the press, he must save both of their reputations...by convincing the world that their passion was the start of a festive royal romance!

HPCNMRA0923

#4149 THE CHRISTMAS THE GREEK CLAIMED HER
From Destitute to Diamonds
by Millie Adams

Maren Hargreave always dreamed of being a princess. When she wins a castle and a crown in a poker game, she's convinced she's found her hard-earned happily-ever-after. But she hadn't realized that in claiming her prize, she's also *marrying* intoxicating billionaire Acastus Diakos!

#4150 HIRED FOR THE BILLIONAIRE'S SECRET SON
by Joss Wood

This summer will be Olivia Cooper's last as a nanny. So she knows that she can't allow herself to get attached to single father Bo Sørenson. Her impending departure *should* make it easier to ignore the billionaire's incendiary gaze...but it only makes it harder to ignore their heat!

#4151 HIS ASSISTANT'S NEW YORK AWAKENING
by Emmy Grayson

Temporary assistant Evolet Grey has precisely the skills and experience needed to help Damon Bradford win the biggest contract in his company's history. But the innocent is also distractingly attractive and testing the iron grip the Manhattan CEO *always* has on his self-control...

#4152 THE FORBIDDEN PRINCESS HE CRAVES
by Lorraine Hall

Sent to claim Elsebet as his brother's wife, Danil Laurentius certainly didn't expect an accident to leave him stranded with the captivating princess. And as she tends to his injuries, the ever-intensifying attraction between them makes him long for the impossible... He wants to claim innocent Elsebet for himself!

YOU CAN FIND MORE INFORMATION ON UPCOMING HARLEQUIN TITLES, FREE EXCERPTS AND MORE AT HARLEQUIN.COM.

HPCNMRB0923

Get 3 FREE REWARDS!

We'll send you 2 FREE Books plus a FREE Mystery Gift.

PRESENTS
His Innocent for One Spanish Night
CAROL MARINELLI

PRESENTS
Bound by the Italian's "I Do"
MICHELLE SMART

FREE
Value Over
$20

Both the **Harlequin® Desire** and **Harlequin Presents®** series feature compelling novels filled with passion, sensuality and intriguing scandals.

YES! Please send me 2 FREE novels from the Harlequin Desire or Harlequin Presents series and my FREE gift (gift is worth about $10 retail). After receiving them, if I don't wish to receive any more books, I can return the shipping statement marked "cancel." If I don't cancel, I will receive 6 brand-new Harlequin Presents Larger-Print books every month and be billed just $6.30 each in the U.S. or $6.49 each in Canada, a savings of at least 10% off the cover price, or 3 Harlequin Desire books (2-in-1 story editions) every month and be billed just $7.83 each in the U.S. and $8.43 each in Canada, a savings of at least 12% off the cover price. It's quite a bargain! Shipping and handling is just 50¢ per book in the U.S. and $1.25 per book in Canada.* I understand that accepting the 2 free books and gift places me under no obligation to buy anything. I can always return a shipment and cancel at any time by calling the number below. The free books and gift are mine to keep no matter what I decide.

Choose one: ☐ **Harlequin Desire**
(225/326 BPA GRNA)

☐ **Harlequin Presents Larger-Print**
(176/376 BPA GRNA)

☐ **Or Try Both!**
(225/326 & 176/376 BPA GRQP)

Name (please print)

Address   Apt. #

City   State/Province   Zip/Postal Code

Email: Please check this box ☐ if you would like to receive newsletters and promotional emails from Harlequin Enterprises ULC and its affiliates. You can unsubscribe anytime.

Mail to the Harlequin Reader Service:
IN U.S.A.: P.O. Box 1341, Buffalo, NY 14240-8531
IN CANADA: P.O. Box 603, Fort Erie, Ontario L2A 5X3

Want to try 2 free books from another series! Call 1-800-873-8635 or visit www.ReaderService.com.

---

*Terms and prices subject to change without notice. Prices do not include sales taxes, which will be charged (if applicable) based on your state or country of residence. Canadian residents will be charged applicable taxes. Offer not valid in Quebec. This offer is limited to one order per household. Books received may not be as shown. Not valid for current subscribers to the Harlequin Presents or Harlequin Desire series. All orders subject to approval. Credit or debit balances in a customer's account(s) may be offset by any other outstanding balance owed by or to the customer. Please allow 4 to 6 weeks for delivery. Offer available while quantities last.

Your Privacy—Your information is being collected by Harlequin Enterprises ULC, operating as Harlequin Reader Service. For a complete summary of the information we collect, how we use this information and to whom it is disclosed, please visit our privacy notice located at corporate.harlequin.com/privacy-notice. From time to time we may also exchange your personal information with reputable third parties. If you wish to opt out of this sharing of your personal information, please visit readerservice.com/consumerschoice or call 1-800-873-8635. **Notice to California Residents**—Under California law, you have specific rights to control and access your data. For more information on these rights and how to exercise them, visit corporate.harlequin.com/california-privacy.

HDHP23

HARLEQUIN
PLUS

Try the best multimedia subscription service for romance readers like you!

Read, Watch and Play.

Experience the easiest way to get the romance content you crave.

Start your **FREE TRIAL** at
<u>www.harlequinplus.com/freetrial</u>.

HARPLUS0123